Thomas Dunn English

The Boy's Book of Battle-lyrics

A Collection of Verses Illustrating Some Notable Events in the History...

Thomas Dunn English

The Boy's Book of Battle-lyrics
A Collection of Verses Illustrating Some Notable Events in the History...

ISBN/EAN: 9783744783057

Printed in Europe, USA, Canada, Australia, Japan

Cover: Foto ©Andreas Hilbeck / pixelio.de

More available books at **www.hansebooks.com**

THE BOY'S BOOK

OF

BATTLE-LYRICS

A COLLECTION OF VERSES ILLUSTRATING SOME NOTABLE EVENTS IN THE
HISTORY OF THE UNITED STATES OF AMERICA, FROM THE COLONIAL
PERIOD TO THE OUTBREAK OF THE SECTIONAL WAR

BY

THOS. DUNN ENGLISH, M.D., LL.D.

WITH HISTORICAL NOTES

AND NUMEROUS ENGRAVINGS OF PERSONS, SCENES, AND PLACES

NEW YORK

HARPER & BROTHERS, FRANKLIN SQUARE

1885

TO

ADOLPH SCHALK, Esq.

AS A RECOGNITION OF MANY YEARS OF UNBROKEN FRIENDSHIP, AND AS A TOKEN
OF ESTEEM FOR HIS MANLINESS AND WORTH

THIS VOLUME IS INSCRIBED BY

THE AUTHOR

PREFACE.

DURING the last twenty-five years my work in verse has been mainly confined to illustrating the history of the United States, with occasional studies of local life and character. Of this, judging by notices of the press, and their appearance in compilations of a patriotic or martial nature, the metrical narratives of battles seem to have been most approved; and it occurred to me that a volume embracing my productions in that line of literary labor might meet with popular favor. My first intention was to take up every notable event, so that the book might be a complete metrical history, and I prepared partly the matter for the purpose, including the capture of the *Serapis* and the achievements of *Old Ironsides*. But I found the volume would be inconveniently large, and I abandoned my plan reluctantly.

The historical sketches prefixed in the proper places will be found full, unless the details are faithfully given in the text, when the introductions are purposely made meagre. In either case they will be found to be accurate, the verses being, as I have styled them, "metrical narratives" rather than poems. In that form, I trust, they more readily impress on the mind of the reader a sense of the patriotism and courage of our forefathers, and give a notion of the nature of the struggle by which these States emerged from a dependent condition to take high rank among the peoples of the world. The story of each event being told in the first person, the style and language are intentionally marked by the peculiarities of the imaginary narrator. And in this connection it will be observed that, because of the nearness of the conflict, the battles of the late sectional war have been avoided, and the two incidents of that period touched on at the close are personal, and not likely to offend even the most sensitive.

T. D. E.

NEWARK, N. J., *July* 30, 1885.

CONTENTS.

ILLUSTRATIONS.

THE BOY'S
BOOK OF BATTLE LYRICS.

DE SOTO'S EXPEDITION.

HERNANDO DE SOTO was of good Spanish family, and started early upon a career of adventure. He was with Francisco Pizarro, and took a prominent part in the conquest of Peru. Some account of his actions while with the Pizarros will be found in Helps's "Spanish Conquest in America." He particularly distinguished himself in the battle which resulted in the conquest of Cuzco, and desired to be the lieutenant of Almagro in the invasion of Chili; but in this he was disappointed. Returning to Spain with much wealth, he married into the Bobadilla family, and became a favorite with the king. Here he conceived the notion of conquering Florida, which he believed to abound in gold and precious stones. Offering to do this at his own expense, the king gave him permission, and at the same time appointed him governor of Cuba. De Soto set sail from Spain in April, 1538, but remained in Cuba some time fitting out his expedition, which did not arrive at Florida until the following year, when it landed at Tampa Bay. His force consisted of twelve hundred men, with four hundred horses, and he took with him a number of domestic animals. In quest of gold, he penetrated the territory now known as the States of Alabama, Georgia, Tennessee, and Mississippi, finally striking the Mississippi River, which he called the Rio Grande, at or near the Lower Chickasaw Bluffs. He found the inhabitants to be quite unlike the Peruvians. He met with a fierce resistance from the natives, and by severe hardships and bloody conflicts found his army very

HERNANDO DE SOTO.

much reduced in numbers. In 1542 De Soto died of a fever. To prevent the mutilation of his body, it was enclosed in a coffin hollowed from the trunk of a tree, and sunk at midnight in the great river. The command then devolved on Moscoso, who escaped with his comrades by way of the river, and reached Mexico in a miserable condition.

It was during this raid, on the 18th of October, 1539, that the battle with the Mobilians was fought. The incidents, so far as they have been gathered from all sources, are faithfully given in the ballad, with one exception. The speech of Tuscaloosa was in the shape of a message, and was delivered by one of his men after the chief had escaped and found refuge in his "palace," which was probably a hut more commodious than the others in the town. The Spaniards, in spite of their superiority of weapons, had much the worst of the affair at one time, and might have been disastrously defeated but for the opportune arrival of Moscoso with the reserve of four hundred fresh men. After that the battle changed to a mere massacre.

The "singing women" described in the text must have been picked Amazons, for the women in general, and children, had been previously sent to a place of refuge by the Mobilians in anticipation of a fight. The slaughter of the poorly armed natives was very great, but the invaders suffered severely. Not only were eighty-two killed, including the nephew and nephew-in-law of the Adelantado (as De Soto was styled), but none of the Spaniards escaped severe wounds. To add to their sufferings, the medicines and surgical appliances, having been placed in the town previous to the breaking out of the conflict, were burned, and all the surgeons but one were killed. De Soto himself received an arrow in his thigh. The missile was not extracted until after the battle, and he was forced to continue the fight standing in his stirrups.

The place of the battle is supposed to be what is now known as Choctaw Bluff, in Clarke County, Alabama.

THE FALL OF MAUBILA.

Hearken the stirring story
  The soldier has to tell,
Of fierce and bloody battle,
  Contested long and well,
Ere walled Maubila, stoutly held,
  Before our forces fell.

Now many years have circled
  Since that October day,
When proudly to Maubila
  De Soto took his way,
With men-at-arms and cavaliers
  In terrible array.

Oh, never sight more goodly
  In any land was seen;
And never better soldiers
  Than those he led have been,
More prompt to handle arquebus,
  Or wield their sabres keen.

The sun was at meridian,
  His hottest rays fell down
Alike on soldier's corselet
  And on the friar's gown;
The breeze was hushed as on we rode
  Right proudly to the town.

First came the bold De Soto,
   In all his manly pride,
The gallant Don Diego,
   His nephew, by his side;
A yard behind Juan Ortiz rode,
   Interpreter and guide.

Baltasar de Gallegos,
   Impetuous, fierce, and hot;
Francisco de Figarro,
   Since by an arrow shot;
And slender Juan de Guzman, who
   In battle faltered not.

Luis Bravo de Xeres,
   That gallant cavalier;
Alonzo de Cormono,
   Whose spirit knew no fear;
The Marquis of Astorga, and
   Vasquez, the cannoneer.

Andres de Vasconcellos,
   Juan Coles, young and fair,
Roma de Cardenoso,
   Him of the yellow hair—
Rode gallant in their bravery,
   Straight to the public square.

And there, in sombre garments,
   Were monks of Cuba four,
Fray Juan de Gallegos,
   And other priests a score,
Who sacramental bread and wine
   And holy relics bore.

And next eight hundred soldiers
   In closest order come,
Some with Biscayan lances,
   With arquebuses some,
Timing their tread to martial notes
   Of trump and fife and drum.

Loud sang the gay Mobilians,
   Light danced their daughters brown :
Sweet sounded pleasant music
   Through all the swarming town ;
But 'mid the joy one sullen brow
   Was lowering with a frown.

The haughty Tuscaloosa,
   The sovereign of the land,
With moody face, and thoughtful,
   Rode at our chief's right hand,
And cast from time to time a glance
   Of hatred at the band.

And when that gay procession
   Made halt to take a rest,
And eagerly the people
   To see the strangers prest,
The frowning King, in wrathful tones,
   De Soto thus addressed :

"To bonds and to dishonor
   By faithless friends trepanned,
For days beside you, Spaniard,
   The ruler of the land
Has ridden as a prisoner,
   Subject to your command.

"He was not born the fetters
   Of baser men to wear,
And tells you this, De Soto,
   Hard though it be to bear—
Let those beware the panther's rage
   Who follow to his lair.

"Back to your isle of Cuba!
   Slink to your den again,
And tell your robber sovereign,
   The mighty lord of Spain,
Whoso would strive this land to win
   Shall find his efforts vain.

"And, save it be your purpose
　Within my realm to die,
Let not your forces linger
　Our deadly anger nigh,
Lest food for vultures and for wolves
　Your mangled forms should lie."

Then, spurning courtly offers,
　He left our chieftain's side,
And crossing the enclosure
　With quick and lengthened stride,
He passed within his palace gates,
　And there our wrath defied.

Now came up Charamilla,
　Who led our troop of spies,
And said unto our captain,
　With tones that showed surprise,
"A mighty force within the town,
　In wait to crush us, lies.

"The babes and elder women
　Were sent at break of day
Into the forest yonder,
　Five leagues or more away;
While in yon huts ten thousand men
　Wait eager for the fray."

"What say ye now, my comrades?"
　De Soto asked his men;
"Shall we, before these traitors,
　Go backward, baffled, then;
Or, sword in hand, attack the foe
　Who crouches in his den?"

Before their loud responses
　Had died upon the ear,
A savage stood before them,
　Who said, in accents clear,
"Ho! robbers base and coward thieves!
　Assassin Spaniards, hear!

"No longer shall our sovereign,
    Born noble, great, and free,
Be led beside your master,
    A shameful sight to see,
While weapons here to strike you down,
    Or hands to grasp them be."

As spoke the brawny savage
    Full wroth our comrades grew—
Baltasar de Gallegos
    His heavy weapon drew,
And dealt the boaster such a stroke
    As clave his body through.

Then rushed the swart Mobilians
    Like hornets from their nest;
Against our bristling lances
    Was bared each savage breast;
With arrow-head and club and stone,
    Upon our band they prest.

"Retreat in steady order!
    But slay them as ye go!"
Exclaimed the brave De Soto,
    And with each word a blow
That sent a savage soul to doom
    He dealt upon the foe.

"Strike well who would our honor
    From spot or tarnish save!
Strike down the haughty Pagan,
    The infidel and slave!
Saint Mary Mother sits above,
    And smiles upon the brave.

"Strike! all my gallant comrades!
    Strike! gentlemen of Spain!
Upon the traitor wretches
    Your deadly anger rain,
Or never to your native land
    Return in pride again!"

Then hosts of angry foemen
 We fiercely held at bay,
Through living walls of Pagans
 We cut our bloody way;
And though by thousands round they swarmed,
 We kept our firm array.

At length they feared to follow;
 We stood upon the plain,
And dressed our shattered columns;
 When, slacking bridle rein,
De Soto, wounded as he was,
 Led to the charge again.

For now our gallant horsemen
 Their steeds again had found,
That had been fastly tethered
 Unto the trees around,
Though some of these, by arrows slain,
 Lay stretched upon the ground.

And as the riders mounted,
 The foe, in joyous tones,
Gave vent to shouts of triumph,
 And hurled a shower of stones;
But soon the shouts were changed to wails,
 The cries of joy to moans.

Down on the scared Mobilians
 The furious rush was led;
Down fell the howling victims
 Beneath the horses' tread;
The angered chargers trod alike
 On dying and on dead.

Back to the wooden ramparts,
 With cut and thrust and blow,
We drove the panting savage,
 The very walls below,
Till those above upon our heads
 Huge rocks began to throw.

Whenever we retreated
  The swarming foemen came—
Their wild and matchless courage
  Put even ours to shame—
Rushing upon our lances' points,
  And arquebuses' flame.

Three weary hours we fought them,
  And often each gave way;
Three weary hours, uncertain
  The fortune of the day;
And ever where they fiercest fought
  De Soto led the fray.

Baltasar de Gallegos
  Right well displayed his might;
His sword fell ever fatal,
  Death rode its flash of light;
And where his horse's head was turned
  The foe gave way in fright.

At length before our daring
  The Pagans had to yield,
And in their stout enclosure
  They sought to find a shield,
And left us, wearied with our toil,
  The masters of the field.

Now worn and spent and weary,
  Our force was scattered round,
Some seeking for their comrades,
  Some seated on the ground,
When sudden fell upon our ears
  A single trumpet's sound.

"Up! ready make for storming!"
  That speaks Moscoso near;
He comes with stainless sabre,
  He comes with spotless spear;
But stains of blood and spots of gore
  Await his weapons here.

Soon, formed in four divisions,
　　Around the order goes—
"To front with battle-axes!
　　No moment for repose.
At signal of an arquebus,
　　Rain on the gates your blows."

Not long that fearful crashing,
　　The gates in splinters fall;
And some, though sorely wounded,
　　Climb o'er the crowded wall;
No rampart's height can keep them back,
　　No danger can appall.

Then redly rained the carnage—
　　None asked for quarter there;
Men fought with all the fury
　　Born of a wild despair;
And shrieks and groans and yells of hate
　　Were mingled in the air.

Four times they backward beat us,
　　Four times our force returned;
We quenched in bloody torrents
　　The fire that in us burned;
We slew who fought, and those who knelt
　　With stroke of sword we spurned.

And what are these new forces,
　　With long, black, streaming hair?
They are the singing maidens
　　Who met us in the square;
And now they spring upon our ranks
　　Like she-wolves from their lair.

Their sex no shield to save them,
　　Their youth no weapon stayed;
De Soto with his falchion
　　A lane amid them made,
And in the skulls of blooming girls
　　Sank battle-axe and blade.

2

Forth came a wingèd arrow,
  And struck our leader's thigh;
The man who sent it shouted,
  And looked to see him die;
The wound but made the tide of rage
  Run twice as fierce and high.

Then cried our stout camp-master,
  "The night is coming down;
Already twilight darkness
  Is casting shadows brown; ·
We would not lack for light on strife
  If once we burned the town."

With that we fired the houses;
  The ranks before us broke;
The fugitives we followed,
  And dealt them many a stroke,
While round us rose the crackling flame,
  And o'er us hung the smoke.

And what with flames around them,
  And what with smoke o'erhead,
And what with cuts of sabre,
  And what with horses' tread,
And what with lance and arquebus,
  The town was filled with dead.

Six thousand of the foemen
  Upon that day were slain,
Including those who fought us
  Outside upon the plain—
Six thousand of the foemen fell,
  And eighty-two of Spain.

Not one of us unwounded
  Came from the fearful fray;
And when the fight was over,
  And scattered round we lay,
Some sixteen hundred wounds we bore
  As tokens of the day.

And through that weary darkness,
　And all that dreary night,
We lay in bitter anguish,
　But never mourned our plight,
Although we watched with eagerness
　To see the morning light.

And when the early dawning
　Had marked the sky with red,
We saw the Moloch incense
　Rise slowly overhead
From smoking ruins and the heaps
　Of charred and mangled dead.

I knew the slain were Pagans,
　While we in Christ were free,
And yet it seemed that moment
　A spirit said to me:
"Henceforth be doomed while life remains
　This sight of fear to see."

And ever since that dawning
　Which chased the night away,
I wake to see the corses
　That thus before me lay;
And this is why in cloistered cell
　I wait my latter day.

Nor an hour's ride from Williamsburg, the seat of the venerable William and Mary College, lie the ruins of Jamestown—part of the tower of the old brick church, piles of bricks, and a number of tombstones with quaint inscriptions, all half overgrown by copse and brambles, being all that remains of the first town of Virginia. At the time of its destruction it could not have been a considerable place. It had the church, a state-house, and a few dwellings built of imported bricks, not more than eighteen in number, if so many. The other houses were probably framed, with some log-huts. Our accounts of the place are meagre, and derived from different sources.

JAMESTOWN AS IT IS.

Nor have we a very full account of the circumstances attending its destruction. So far as they are gathered they amount to this: Sir William Berkeley, who at the outset of his administration had been a good governor, was displaced during the troubles at home, and when he returned, had been soured, and proved to be exacting and tyrannical. Refusing to allow a force to be led against the Indian enemy, the people took it in their own hands. Berkeley had a show of right in the matter. Indian chiefs had come to John Washington, the great-grandfather of George Washington, to treat of peace. Washington was colonel of Westmoreland County, and he had these messengers killed. Berkeley was indignant. "They came in peace," said he, "and I would have sent them in peace if they had killed my father and mother." The bloody act aroused the vengeance of the Indians, and they fell on the frontier and massacred men, women, and children. The governor considered it a just retribution, and refused authority for reprisals. The people, who had no notion that innocent parties should suffer for one man's barbarous deed, organized. They chose Nathaniel Bacon, who was a popular young lawyer, for their leader, and asked Berkeley to confirm him. This request was refused. When some new murders by the Indians occurred, Bacon marched against the enemy, and the governor proclaimed him and his men rebels. When Bacon returned in triumph he was elected a member of the assembly from Henrico County, and that assembly passed laws of such a popular nature that Berkeley, in alarm, left Jamestown. Bacon raised a force of five hundred men, and Berkeley, who possessed high personal courage, met them alone. He uncovered his breast and said, "A fair mark. Shoot!" But when Bacon explained that he merely asked a commission, the people being in peril from the enemy, this was granted; but no sooner had Bacon departed to attack the Indians than Berkeley withdrew to the Eastern Shore, where he collected a force of a thousand men from Accomac, to whom he offered pay and plunder. With these he returned to Jamestown, and proclaimed Bacon and his adherents rebels and traitors.

Bacon, having severely chastised the Indians, returned; but only a few of his followers remained. This was in September, 1676. He laid regular siege to Jamestown; but, as his force was so weak, he feared a sortie by overwhelming numbers. To avert this, and gain time to complete his works, he resorted to stratagem. By means of a picked party, sent at night, he captured the wives of the leading inhabitants. These, the next day, he placed on the summit of a small work in sight of the town, and kept them thus exposed until he had completed his lines, when he released them. Berkeley sallied out, and was repulsed. He could not depend on his own men, and that night he retired in his vessels. Bacon entered the town next morning, and after consultation, it was agreed to destroy the place. At seven o'clock in the evening, the torch was applied, and in the morning the tower of the church and a few chimneys were all that were left standing.

A number of Berkeley's men now joined Bacon, who was undisputed master of the colony; but dying shortly after, his party dispersed. Berkeley, reinstated, took signal vengeance and executed about twenty of the most prominent of Bacon's friends. He was only stopped by the positive orders of the King, by whom he was removed, and Lord Culpepper, almost as great a tyrant, sent in his room.

THE BURNING OF JAMESTOWN.

Mad Berkeley believed, with his gay cavaliers,
    And the ruffians he brought from the Accomac shore,
He could ruffle our spirit by rousing our fears,
    And lord it again as he lorded before:
        It was—"Traitors, be dumb!"
        And—"Surrender, ye scum!"
And that Bacon, our leader, was rebel, he swore.

A rebel? Not he! He was true to the throne;
    For the King, at a word, he would lay down his life;
But to listen unmoved to the piteous moan
    When the redskin was plying the hatchet and knife,
        And shrink from the fray,
        Was not the man's way—
It was Berkeley, not Bacon, who stirred up the strife.

On the outer plantations the savages burst,
  And scattered around desolation and woe;
And Berkeley, possessed by some spirit accurst,
  Forbade us to deal for our kinsfolk a blow;
      Though when, weapons in hand,
      We made our demand,
He sullenly suffered our forces to go.

Then while we were doing our work for the crown,
  And risking our lives in the perilous fight,
He sent lying messengers out, up and down,
  To denounce us as outlaws—mere malice and spite;
      Then from Accomac's shore
      Brought a thousand or more,
Who swaggered the country around, day and night.

Returning in triumph, instead of reward
  For the marches we made and the battles we won,
There were threats of the fetters or bullet or sword—
  Were these a fair guerdon for what we had done?
      When this madman abhorred
      Appealed to the sword,
And our leader said—"fight!" did he think we would run?

Battle-scarred, and a handful of men as we were,
  We feared not to combat with lord or with lown,
So we took the old wretch at his word—that was fair;
  But he dared not come out from his hold in the town,
      Where he lay with his men,
      Like a wolf in his den;
And in siege of the place we sat steadily down.

He made a fierce sally—his force was so strong
  He thought the mere numbers would put us to flight—
But we met in close column his ruffianly throng,
  And smote it so sore that we filled him with fright;
      Then while ready we lay
      For the storming next day,
He embarked in his ships, and escaped in the night.

The place was our own; could we hold it? why, no!
  Not if Berkeley should gather more force and return;

But one course was left us to baffle the foe—
   The birds would not come if the nest we should burn;
      So the red, crackling fire
      Climbed to roof-top and spire,
A lesson for black-hearted Berkeley to learn.

That our torches destroyed what our fathers had raised
   On that beautiful isle, is it matter of blame?
That the houses we dwelt in, the church where they praised
   The God of our Fathers, we gave to the flame?
      That we smiled when there lay
      Smoking ruins next day,
And nothing was left of the town but its name?

We won; but we lost when brave Nicholas died;
   The spirit that nerved us was gone from us then;
And Berkeley came back in his arrogant pride
   To give to the gallows the best of our men;
      But while the grass grows
      And the clear water flows,
The town shall not rise from its ashes again.

So, you come for your victim! I'm ready; but, pray,
   Ere I go, some good fellow a full goblet bring.
Thanks, comrade! Now hear the last words I shall say
   With the last drink I take. Here's a health to the King,
      Who reigns o'er a land
      Where, against his command,
The rogues rule and ruin, and honest men swing.

In 1703, Colonel Johannis Schuyler, grandfather of the Revolutionary general, Philip Schuyler, and uncle of the still more famous Peter Schuyler, so distinguished in the Franco-Canadian war, was mayor of Albany. From some Indians trading there he obtained information that an attack on Deerfield was planned from Canada. He sent word to the villagers, who prepared to meet it. The design not having been carried out that summer, the people of Deerfield supposed it to have been abandoned, and dismissed their fears. The next year Vaudreuil, the governor of Canada, despatched a force of three hundred French and Indians against the place. The expedition was under the command of Hertel de Rouville, the son of an almost equally famous partisan officer. With him were four of his brothers. The raiders came by way of Lake Champlain to the Onion River—then called the French—up which they advanced, and passed on, marching on the ice, until they were near Deerfield. The minister of the place, the Rev. Mr. Williams, unlike the rest of the townsmen, had feared an attack for some time, and on his application the provincial government had sent a guard of twenty men. There were two or three block-houses, and around these some palisades. De Rouville came near the town before daylight on the 29th of February, and learned by his spies the condition of the place. Finding that the sentinels had gone to sleep two hours before dawn, and that the snow had drifted in one place so as to cover the palisades, he led a rush, and then dispersed his men in small parties through

ELEAZER WILLIAMS.

the town to make a simultaneous attack. The place was carried, with the exception of one garrison-house which held out successfully. Forty-seven of the inhabitants were killed, and nearly all the rest captured. The enemy, failing to reduce the single block-house, retreated with their prisoners, taking up their march for Canada. A band of colonists was hurriedly raised, and pursued De Rouville; but they were beaten off after a sharp fight. A hundred and twelve prisoners were carried away. A few were killed on the march; the greater part were ransomed, and returned in about two years.

Among the prisoners was the Rev. Mr. Williams. His wife, unable to keep up with the party, was killed on the second day by her captor. Two of his children had been killed during the sack. One of his daughters, Eunice, while in captivity was converted to the Catholic religion, and married with an Indian. She entirely adopted Indian habits, and was pleased with her life. Afterwards she occasionally visited her friends in New England, but no persuasion would induce her to remain there. A chronicler states, with a comical mixture of surprise and indignation, "She uniformly persisted in wearing her blankets and counting her beads." One of her descendants was a highly respected clergyman, the Rev. Eleazer Williams, who died a few years since, and who during life became the subject of controversy. Mr. Hansen wrote an article, and finally a book, "The Lost Prince," to prove that Mr. Williams was really the missing Dauphin, Louis the Sixteenth. A look at the clergyman's portrait shows the half-breed features quite distinctly, though the claim was plausibly put, and for a time had its ardent supporters.

THE SACK OF DEERFIELD.

Of the onset fear-inspiring, and the firing and the pillage
　　Of our village, when De Rouville with his forces on us fell,
When, ere dawning of the morning, with no death-portending warning,
　　With no token shown or spoken, came the foemen, hear me tell.

High against the palisadoes, on the meadows, banks, and hill-sides,
　　At the rill-sides, over fences, lay the lingering winter snow;
And so high by tempest rifted, at our pickets it was drifted,
　　That its frozen crust was chosen as a bridge to bear the foe.

We had set at night a sentry, lest an entry, while the sombre
　　Heavy slumber was upon us, by the Frenchman should be made;
But the faithless knave we posted, though of wakefulness he boasted,
　　'Stead of keeping watch was sleeping, and his solemn trust betrayed.

Than our slumber none profounder; never sounder fell on sleeper,
　　Never deeper sleep its shadow cast on dull and listless frames;
But it fled before the crashing of the portals, and the flashing,
　　And the soaring, and the roaring, and the crackling of the flames.

Fell the shining hatchets quickly 'mid the thickly crowded women,
　　Growing dim in crimson currents from the pulses of the brain;
Rained the balls from firelocks deadly, till the melted snow ran redly
　　With the glowing torrent flowing from the bodies of the slain.

I, from pleasant dreams awaking at the breaking of my casement,
　　With amazement saw the foemen quickly enter where I lay;
Heard my wife and children's screaming, as the hatchets woke their
　　　　dreaming,
　　Heard their groaning and their moaning as their spirits passed away.

'Twas in vain I struggled madly as the sadly sounding pleading
　　Of my bleeding, dying darlings fell upon my tortured ears;

'Twas in vain I wrestled, raging, fight against their numbers waging,
  Crowding round me there they bound me, while my manhood sank
    in tears.

At the spot to which they bore me, no one o'er me watched or warded;
  There unguarded, bound and shivering, on the snow I lay alone;
Watching by the firelight ruddy, as the butchers dark and bloody
  Slew the nearest friends and dearest to my memory ever known.

And it seemed, as rose the roaring blaze, up soaring, redly streaming
  O'er the gleaming snow around me through the shadows of the night,
That the figures flitting fastly were the fiends at revels ghastly,
  Madly urging on the surging, seething billows of the fight.

Suddenly my gloom was lightened, hope was heightened, though the
    shrieking,
  Malice-wreaking, ruthless wretches death were scattering to and fro;
For a knife lay there—I spied it, and a tomahawk beside it
  Glittering brightly, buried lightly, keen edge upward, in the snow.

Naught knew I how came they thither, nor from whither; naught to
    me then
  If the heathen dark, my captors, dropped those weapons there or no;
Quickly drawn o'er axe-edge lightly, cords were cut that held me tightly,
  Then, with engines of my vengeance in my hands, I sought the foe.

Oh, what anger dark, consuming, fearful, glooming, looming horrid,
  Lit my forehead, draped my figure, leapt with fury from my glance;
'Midst the foemen rushing frantic, to their sight I seemed gigantic,
  Like the motion of the ocean, like a tempest my advance.

Stoutest of them all, one savage left the ravage round and faced me;
  Fury braced me, for I knew him—he my pleading wife had slain.
Huge he was, and brave and brawny, but I met the slayer tawny,
  And with rigorous blow, and vigorous, clove his tufted skull in twain—
  Madly dashing down the crashing bloody hatchet in his brain.

As I brained him rose their calling, "Lo! appalling from yon meadow
  The Monedo of the white man comes with vengeance in his train!"
As they fled, my blows Titanic falling fast increased their panic,
  Till their shattered forces scattered widely o'er the snowy plain.

"HUGE HE WAS, AND BRAVE AND BRAWNY, BUT I MET THE SLAYER TAWNY."

Stern De Rouville then their error, born of terror, soon dispersing,
 Loudly cursing them for folly, roused their pride with words of scorn;
Peering cautiously they knew me, then by numbers overthrew me;
 Fettered surely, bound securely, there again I lay forlorn.

Well I knew their purpose horrid, on each forehead it was written—
 Pride was smitten that their bravest had retreated at my ire;
For the rest the captives durance, but for me there was assurance
 Of the tortures known to martyrs—of the terrible death by fire.

Then I felt, though horror-stricken, pulses quicken as the swarthy
 Savage, or the savage Frenchman, fiercest of the cruel band,

Darted in and out the shadows, through the shivered palisadoes,
  Death-blows dealing with unfeeling heart and never-sparing hand.

Soon the sense of horror left me, and bereft me of all feeling;
  Soon, revealing all my early golden moments, memory came;
Showing how, when young and sprightly, with a footstep falling lightly,
  I had pondered as I wandered on the maid I loved to name.

Her, so young, so pure, so dove-like, that the love-like angels whom a
  Sweet aroma circles ever wheresoe'er they wave their wings,
Felt with her the air grow sweeter, felt with her their joy completer,
  Felt their gladness swell to madness, silent grow their silver strings.

Then I heard her voice's murmur breathing summer, while my spirit
  Leaned to hear it and to drink it like a draught of pleasant wine;
Felt her head upon my shoulder drooping as my love I told her,
  Felt the utterly pleased flutter of her heart respond to mine.

Then I saw our darlings clearly that more nearly linked our gladness;
  Saw our sadness as a lost one sank from pain to happy rest;
Mingled tears with hers, and chid her, bade her by our love consider
  How our dearest now was nearest to the blessed Master's breast.

I had lost that wife so cherished, who had perished, passed from being,
  In my seeing—I, unable to protect her or defend;   .
At that thought dispersed those fancies, born of woe-begotten trances,
  While unto me came the gloomy present hour my heart to rend.

For I heard the firelocks ringing, fiercely flinging forth the whirring,
  Blood-preferring leaden bullets from a garrisoned abode;
There it stood so grim and lonely, speaking of its tenants only,
  When the furious leaden couriers from its loop-holes fastly rode.

And the seven who kept it stoutly, though devoutly triumph praying,
  Ceased not slaying, trusting somewhat to their firelocks and their wives;
For while they the house were holding, balls the wives were quickly
    moulding—
  Neither fearful, wild, nor tearful, toiling earnest for their lives.

Onward rushed each dusky leaguer, hot and eager, but the seven
  Rained the levin from their firelocks as the Pagans forward pressed;

" FOR WHILE THEY THE HOUSE WERE HOLDING, BALLS THE WIVES WERE QUICKLY MOULDING."

Melting at that murderous firing, back that baffled foe retiring,
    Left there lying, dead or dying, ten, their bravest and their best.

Rose the red sun, straightly throwing from his glowing disk his bright-
    ness
    On the whiteness of the snow-drifts and the ruins of the town—
On those houses well defended, where the foe in vain expended
    Ball and powder, standing prouder, smoke-begrimed and scarred and
    brown.

Not for us those rays shone fairly, tinting rarely dawning early
    With the pearly light and glistering of the March's snowy morn ;

Some were wounded, some were weary, some were sullen, all were dreary,
  As the sorrow of that morrow shed its cloud of woe forlorn.

Then we heard De Rouville's orders, "To the borders!" and the dismal,
  Dark, abysmal fate before us opened widely as he spoke;
But we heard a shout in distance—into fluttering existence,
  Brief but splendid, quickly ended, at the sound our hopes awoke.

'Twas our kinsmen armed and ready, sweeping steady to the nor'ward,
  Pressing forward fleet and fearless, though in scanty force they came—
Cried De Rouville, grimly speaking, "Is't our captives you are seeking?
  Well, with iron we environ them, and wall them round with flame.

"With the toil of blood we won them, we've undone them with our bravery;
  Off to slavery, then, we carry them or leave them lifeless here.
Foul my shame so far to wander, and my soldiers' blood to squander
  'Mid the slaughter free as water, should our prey escape us clear.

"Off, ye scum of peasants Saxon, and your backs on Frenchmen turning,
  To our burning, dauntless courage proper tribute promptly pay;
Do you come to seize and beat us? Are you here to slay and eat us?
  If your meat be Gaul and Mohawk, we will starve you out to-day."

How my spirit raged to hear him, standing near him bound and helpless!
  Never whelpless tigress fiercer howled at slayer of her young,
When secure behind his engines, he has baffled her of vengeance,
  Than did I there, forced to lie there while his bitter taunts he flung.

For I heard each leaden missile whirr and whistle from the trusty
  Firelock rusty, brought there after long-time absence from the strife,
And was forced to stand in quiet, with my warm blood running riot,
  When for power to give an hour to battle I had bartered life.

All in vain they thus had striven; backward driven, beat and broken,
  Leaving token of their coming in the dead around the dell,
They retreated—well it served us! their retreat from death preserved us,
  Though the order for our murder from the dark De Rouville fell.

As we left our homes in ashes, through the lashes of the sternest
  Welled the earnest tears of anguish for the dear ones passed away;
Sick at heart and heavily loaded, though with cruel blows they goaded,
  Sorely cumbered, miles we numbered four alone that weary day.

They were tired themselves of tramping, for encamping they were ready,
　Ere the steady twilight newer pallor threw upon the snow ;
So they built them huts of branches, in the snow they scooped out trenches,
　Heaped up firing, then, retiring, let us sleep our sleep of woe.

By the wrist—and by no light hand—to the right hand of a painted,
　Murder-tainted, loathsome Pagan, with a jeer, I soon was tied ;
And the one to whom they bound me, 'mid the scoffs of those around me,
　Bowing to me, mocking, drew me down to slumber at his side.

As for me, be sure I slept not : slumber crept not on my senses ;
　Less intense is lovers' musing than a captive's bent on ways
To escape from fearful thralling, and a death by fire appalling ;
　So, unsleeping, I was keeping on the Northern Star my gaze.

There I lay—no muscle stirring, mind unerring, thought unswerving,
　Body nerving, till a death-like, breathless slumber fell around ;
Then my right hand cautious stealing, o'er my bed-mate's person feeling,
　Till each finger stooped to linger on the belt his waist that bound.

'Twas his knife—the handle clasping, firmly grasping, forth I drew it,
　Clinging to it firm, but softly, with a more than robber's art ;
As I drove it to its utter length of blade, I heard the flutter
　Of a snow-bird—ah ! 'twas *no* bird ! 'twas the flutter of my heart.

Then I cut the cord that bound me, peered around me, rose uprightly,
　Stepped as lightly as a lover on his blessed bridal day ;
Swiftly as my need inclined me, kept the bright North Star behind me,
　And, ere dawning of the morning, I was twenty miles away.

THE Lewis family seem to have occupied a position as prominent, and to have been as much identified with the local history of the Colony of Virginia, as the Schuyler family with New York and New Jersey. The John Lewis who is the hero of the ballad, though less known than Andrew, who overcame Cornstalk at Point Pleasant, and who was thought of before Washington for command of the Continental army, was nevertheless a remarkable man. He was of that Scotch-Irish race which settled the western part of Pennsylvania and Virginia, and spread into North Carolina, Kentucky, and Tennessee, making a people distinct in dialect and character, and preserving a number of North of Ireland customs to this day. John was a famous Indian fighter in his youth. At the time of the defence described in the ballad he had grown quite old. His wife, who came of a fighting family, aided him to drive off the enemy, who would have endured almost any loss to have secured him as a prisoner. They hated him intensely, and with just cause. When red clover was introduced in that section, the savages believed that it was the white clover, dyed in the blood of the Indians killed by the Lewises.

THE FIGHT OF JOHN LEWIS.

I.

To be captain and host in the fortress,
　　To keep his assailants at bay,
To battle a hundred of Mingos,
　　A score of the foemen to slay—
John Lewis did so in Augusta,
　　In days that have long gone away.

And I will maintain on my honor,
　　That never by poet was told
A fight half so worthy of mention,
　　Since those which the annals of old
Record as the wonderful doings
　　Of knights and of Paladins bold—

Ay, though about Richards or Rolands,
　　Or any such terrible dogs,
Who were covered with riveted armor
　　Of the pattern of Magog's and Gog's,
While Lewis wore brown linsey-woolsey,
　　And lived in a cabin of logs.

II.

They had started in arms from Fort Lewis,
  One morn, in pursuit of the foe;
They had gone at the hour before dawning,
  Over hills and through valleys below,
Leaving there, with the children and women,
  John Lewis, unfitted to go.

Too weak for the toil of the travel,
  Too old in the fight to have part,
Too feeble to stalk through the forest,
  Yet fierce as a storm in his heart—
He chafed that without him his neighbors
  Should thus to the battle-field start.

"How well," he exclaimed, "I remember,
  When over my threshold there came
A proud and an arrogant noble
  To proffer me outrage and shame,
To bring to my household dishonor,
  And offer my roof to the flame—

"I rose up erect in my manhood,
  The sword of my fathers I drew;
In spite of his many retainers,
  That arrogant noble I slew,
And then, with revenge fully sated,
  Bade home and my country adieu.

"Ah, were I but stronger and younger,
  How eager and ready, to-day,
I would move with the bravest and boldest,
  As first in the perilous fray;
But now, while the rest do the fighting,
  A laggard, with women I stay."

The women they laughed when they heard him,
  But one answered kindly, and said,
"Uncle John, though the days have departed
  When our chiefest your orders obeyed,
Yet still, at the name of John Lewis,
  The Mingos grow weak and afraid.

3

"Yon block-house were weak as a shelter,
  Were blood-thirsty savages near,
Yet while you are at hand to defend us,
  Not one of us women would fear,
But laugh at their malice and anger,
  Though hundreds of foemen were here."

Away to their work went the women—
  Some drove off the cattle to browse;
Some swept from the hearth the cold embers;
  Some started to milking the cows;
While Lewis went into the block-house,
  And said unto Maggie, his spouse,

"Ah, would they but come to besiege me,
  They'd find, though no more on the trail
I may move as in earlier manhood—
  Though thus, in my weakness, I rail—
That to handle the death-dealing rifle,
  These fingers of mine would not fail."

III.

John Lewis, thy vaunt shall be tested,
  John Lewis, thy boast shall be tried;
Two maidens are with thee for shelter,
  The wife of thy youth by thy side;
And thy foemen pour down like a river
  When spring-rains have swollen its tide.

They come from the depths of the forest,
  They scatter in rage through the dell,
Five score, led by young Kiskepila,
  And leap to their work with a yell,
Like the shrieks of an army of demons
  Let loose from their prison in hell.

Oh, then there were shrieking and wailing,
  And praying for mercy in vain;
Through the skulls of the hapless and helpless
  The hatchet sank in to the brain;
And the slayers tore, fastly and fiercely,
  The scalps from the heads of the slain.

By the ruthless and blood-thirsty Mingos
  Encompassed on every side,
Cut off from escape to the block-house,
  No way from pursuers to hide,
With a prayer to the Father Almighty,
  Unresisting, the innocents died.

John Lewis, in torture of spirit,
  Beheld them ply hatchet and knife,
And said, "Were I younger and stronger,
  And fit as of yore for the strife!
Oh, had I from now until sunset
  The vigor of earlier life!"

IV.

Unsated with horror and carnage,
  Their arms all bedabbled with gore,
The foemen, with purpose determined,
  Assembled the block-house before,
And their leader exclaimed, "Ho! John Lewis!
  The Mingos are here at the door.

"The mystery-men of our nation
  Declare that the blood you have shed
Has fallen so fastly and freely
  The white clover flowers have grown red;
And that never will safety be with us
  Till you are a prisoner or dead.

"So keep us not waiting, old panther;
  Come forth from your log-bounded lair!
If in quiet you choose to surrender,
  Your life at the least we will spare;
But refuse, and the scalping-knife bloody
  Shall circle ere long in your hair."

"Cowards all," answered Lewis; "now mark me.
  Beside me are good rifles three;
I can sight on the bead true as ever,
  My wife she can load, do you see?
You may war upon children and women,
  Beware how you war upon me."

They rushed on the block-house in anger;
   They rushed on the block-house in vain;
Swift sped the round ball from the rifle—
   The foremost invader was slain;
And ere they could bear back the fallen,
   The dead of the foemen were twain.

So, firmly and sternly he fought them,
   And steadily, six hours and more;
And often they rushed to the combat,
   And often in terror forbore;
But never they wounded John Lewis,
   Who slew of their number a score.

Ah, woe to your white hair, old hunter,
   When powder and bullet be done;
You shall die by the slowest of tortures
   When these shall the battle have won.
Look then to your Maker for mercy,
   The Mingo will surely have none.

V.

A shout! 'tis the neighbors returning!
   Now, Mingos, in terror fall back!
It is well that your sinews are lusty,
   And well that no vigor ye lack;
He is best who in motion is fleetest
   When the white man is out on his track.

Oh, then fell around them a terror;
   Oh, then how the enemy ran;
For each hunter, in chosen position,
   With coolness of vengeance began
To take a good aim with his rifle,
   And send a sure shot to his man.

Oh, then there was racing and chasing,
   And fastly they hurried away;
They feared at those husbands and fathers,
   And dared not stand boldly at bay;
And in front of his men, Kiskepila
   Ran slightly the fastest they say.

And well for the lives of the wretches
   They fly from the brunt of the fight;
And well for their lives that around them
   Are falling the shadows of night;
For life is in distance and darkness,
   And death in the nearness and light.

But deep was the woe of the hunters,
   And dark was the cloud o'er their life;
For some had been riven of children,
   And some of both children and wife;
And woe to the barbarous Mingo,
   If either should meet him in strife.

John Lewis said, calmly and coldly,
   When gazing that eve on the slain—
"We will bury our dead on the morrow,
   But let these red rascals remain;
And the wandering wolves and the buzzards
   Will not of our kindness complain."

Years after, when men called John Lewis
   As brave as a brave man could be,
He lit him his pipe made of corn-cob,
   And drawing a draught long and free—
"The red rascals kept me quite busy
   With pulling the trigger," said he.

"And though I got slightly the better
   Of insolent foes in the strife,
I may as well own that my triumph
   Was due unto Maggie, my wife;
For had she not loaded expertly,
   The Mingos had reft us of life.

"And through all that terrible combat
   She never was scared at the din;
But carefully loaded each rifle,
   And prophesied that we would win—
Yet why should she tremble? her fathers
   Were the terrible lords of Loch Linn."

John Lewis commanded the fortress;
  John Lewis was army as well;
John Lewis was master of ordnance;
  John Lewis he fought as I tell;
And, gathered long since to his fathers,
  John Lewis lies low in the dell.

But a braver old man, or a better,
  Was never yet known to exist;
Not even in olden Augusta,
  Where good men who died were not missed,
For the very particular reason—
  Good men then were plenty, I wist.

THE FIRST BLOOD DRAWN.

CLARK'S HOUSE, LEXINGTON.

In the spring of 1775, General Gage, commanding the royal troops in Boston, determined to seize the arms and stores which the colonists had gathered at Concord. At midnight, on the eighteenth of April, he sent eight hundred men, grenadiers and light infantry, under Lieutenant-colonel Smith and Major Pitcairn, for that purpose. They landed quietly at Phipps's Farm, and to insure secrecy arrested all they met on the march. General Warren, however, knew of it, and sent Paul Revere with the news to John Hancock and Samuel Adams, both of whom were at Clark's House, in Lexington. Revere spread the alarm. By two o'clock in the morning a company of minute-men met on the green at Lexington, and after forming were dismissed, with orders to re-assemble on call. In the mean while the ringing of bells and firing of guns told the British that their movements were known. Smith detached the greater part of his force, under Pitcairn, with orders to push on to Concord. As they approached Lexington they came upon the minute-men, who had hastily turned out again. A pause ensued, both parties hesitating. Then Pitcairn called on them to disperse. Not being obeyed, he moved his troops, and a few random shots having been exchanged, gave the order to fire. Four of the minute-men fell at the volley, and the rest dispersed. As the British fired again, while the Americans were retreating, some shots were returned. Four of the Americans were killed, and three of the British were wounded. Joined by Smith and his men, the British pushed on to Concord.

But the country was now thoroughly aroused. A strong party of militia, though less in force than the enemy, had been gathered under the command of Colonel Barrett, an old soldier, who had served with Amherst and Abercrombie. Under his direction most of the stores were removed to a place of safety. At seven in the morning the British arrived at the place, and found two companies of militia on the Common. These retreated to some high

SAMUEL ADAMS.

THE LEXINGTON MASSACRE.—[FROM AN OLD PRINT.]

ground about a mile back. The enemy then occupied the town, secured the bridges, destroyed what stores had been left, and broke off the trunnions of three 24-pound cannon. They also fired the town. Meanwhile the forces of the Americans increased to four companies. After consultation, Major Buttrick was sent with a detachment to attack the enemy at the North Bridge. Here a fight ensued. Two Americans and three British were killed, and several on both sides were wounded. The British detachment retreated, and the Americans took the bridge. The enemy, seeing Americans continually arriving, were alarmed, and Smith ordered a speedy return to Boston, throwing out flanking parties on the march. But it seemed as though armed men sprang from every house and barn, or were lurking behind every rock and tree. Shots came from every quarter, and were mostly fatal. Charges had no effect. Driven from one point, fresh assailants came from another. It seemed as though the entire detachment would be slain or captured.

Gage received word of the swarming of the minute-men and the peril of his troops, and sent a brigade, with light artillery, under Lord Percy, to reinforce Smith. This reached within a half mile of Lexington at three o'clock in the afternoon, and forming a hollow square around the wearied soldiers, allowed them a short time for rest and

JOHN HANCOCK.

FIGHT AT THE BRIDGE.

refreshment. Then the whole body began its return march, destroying houses and doing other mischief on the way. The country was now up, the provincial troops came from all quarters, and it was a general running engagement. At Prospect Hill there was a sharp fight. Percy seemed in danger of being cut off; but another and stronger reinforcement arriving, he was enabled to reach Boston.

THE FIGHT AT LEXINGTON.

Tugged the patient, panting horses, as the coulter keen and thorough,
By the careful farmer guided, cut the deep and even furrow;
Soon the mellow mould in ridges, straightly pointing as an arrow,
Lay to wait the bitter vexing of the fierce, remorseless harrow—
Lay impatient for the seeding, for the growing and the reaping,
All the richer and the readier for the quiet winter-sleeping.

At his loom the pallid weaver, with his feet upon the treadles,
Watched the threads alternate rising, with the lifting of the heddles—
Not admiring that, so swiftly, at his eager fingers' urging,
Flew the bobbin-loaded shuttle 'twixt the filaments diverging;

Only labor dull and cheerless in the work before him seeing,
As the warp and woof uniting brought the figures into being.

Roared the fire before the bellows; glowed the forge's dazzling crater;
Rang the hammers on the anvil, both the lesser and the greater;
Fell the sparks around the smithy, keeping rhythm to the clamor,
To the ponderous blows and clanging of each unrelenting hammer;
While the diamonds of labor, from the curse of Adam borrowed,
Glittered in a crown of honor on each iron-beater's forehead.

Through the air there came a whisper, deepening quickly into thunder,
How the deed was done that morning that would rend the realm asunder;
How at Lexington the Briton mingled causeless crime with folly,
And a king endangered empire by an ill-considered volley.
Then each heart beat quick for vengeance, as the anger-stirring story
Told of brethren and of neighbors lying corses stiff and gory.

Stops the plough and sleeps the shuttle, stills the blacksmith's noisy
        hammer,
Come the farmer, smith, and weaver, with a wrath too deep for clamor;
But their fiercely purposed doing every glance they give avouches,
As they handle rusty firelocks, powder-horns, and bullet-pouches;
As they hurry from the workshops, from the fields, and from the forges,
Venting curses deep and bitter on the latest of the Georges.

Matrons gather at the portals—some with children round them grouping,
Some are filled with exultation, some are sad of soul and drooping—
Gazing at our hasty levies as they march unskilled but steady,
Or prepare their long-kept firelocks, for the combat making ready—
Mingling smiles with tears, and praying for our men and those who lead
        them,
That the gracious Lord of battles to a triumph sure may speed them.

I was but a beardless stripling on that chilly April morning,
When the church-bells backward ringing, to the minute-men gave warning;
But I seized my father's weapons—he was dead who one time bore them—
And I swore to use them stoutly, or to nevermore restore them;
Bade farewell to sister, mother, and to one than either dearer,
Then departed as the firing told of red-coats drawing nearer.

On the Britons came from Concord—'twas a name of mocking omen;
Concord nevermore existed 'twixt our people and the foemen—

On they came in haste from Concord, where a few had stood to fight them,
Where they failed to conquer Buttrick, who had stormed the bridge despite
        them;
On they came, the tools of tyrants, 'mid a people who abhorred them;
They had done their master's bidding, and we purposed to reward them.

We, at Meriam's Corner posted, heard the fifing and the drumming
In the distance creeping onward, which prepared us for their coming;
Soon we saw the lines of scarlet, their advance to music timing,
When our captain quickly bade us pick our flints and freshen priming.
There our little band of freemen, couched in silent ambush lying,
Watched the forces, full eight hundred, as they came with colors flying.

BATTLE-GROUND AT CONCORD.

'Twas a goodly sight to see them; but we heeded not its splendor,
For we felt their martial bearing hate within our hearts engender,
Kindling fire within our spirits, though our eyes a moment watered,
As we thought on Moore and Hadley, and their brave companions
        slaughtered;
And we swore to deadly vengeance for the fallen to devote them,
And our rage grew hotter, hotter, as our well-aimed bullets smote them.

Then, in overpowering numbers, charging bayonet, came their flankers:
We were driven as the ships are, by a tempest, from their anchors.

MERIAM'S CORNER, ON THE LEXINGTON ROAD.

But we loaded while retreating, and, regaining other shelter,
Saw their proudest on the highway in their life's blood fall and welter ;
Saw them fall, or dead or wounded, at our fire so quick and deadly,
While the dusty road was moistened with the torrent raining redly.

From behind the mounds and fences poured the bullets thickly, fastly ;
From ravines and clumps of coppice leaped destruction grim and ghastly ;
All around our leaguers hurried, coming hither, going thither,
Yet, when charged on by their forces, disappearing, none knew whither ;
Buzzed around the hornets ever, newer swarms each moment springing,
Breaking, rising, and returning, yet continually stinging.

HALT OF TROOPS NEAR ELISHA JONES'S HOUSE.

When to Hardy's Hill their weary, waxing-fainter footsteps brought them,
There again the stout Provincials brought the wolves to bay and
    fought them ;
And though often backward beaten, still returned the foe to follow,
Making forts of every hill-top, and redoubts of every hollow.
Hunters came from every farm-house, joining eagerly to chase them—
They had boasted far too often that we ne'er would dare to face them.

THE PROVINCIALS ON PUNKATASSET.

How they staggered, how they trembled, how they panted at pursuing,
How they hurried broken columns that had marched to their undoing ;
How their stout commander, wounded, urged along his frightened forces,
That had marked their fearful progress by their comrades' bloody corses ;
How they rallied, how they faltered, how in vain returned our firing,
While we hung upon their footsteps with a zealousness untiring.

With nine hundred came Lord Percy, sent by startled Gage to meet them,
And he scoffed at those who suffered such a horde of boors to beat them ;
But his scorn was changed to anger, when on front and flank were falling,
From the fences, walls, and roadside, drifts of leaden hail appalling ;
And his picked and chosen soldiers, who had never shrunk in battle,
Hurried quicker in their panic when they heard the firelocks rattle.

Tell it not in Gath, Lord Percy, never Ascalon let hear it,
That you fled from those you taunted as devoid of force and spirit ;
That the blacksmith, weaver, farmer, leaving forging, weaving, tillage,
Fully paid with coin of bullets base marauders for their pillage ;
They, you said, would fly in terror, Britons and their bayonets shunning ;
But the loudest of the boasters proved the foremost in the running.

Then round Prospect Hill they hurried, where we followed and assailed
    them ;
They had stout and tireless muscles, or their limbs had surely failed
    them ;
Stood abashed the bitter Tories, as the women loudly wondered
That a crowd of scurvy rebels chased to hold eleven hundred—
Chased to hold eleven hundred, grenadiers both light and heavy,
Leading Percy, of the Border, on a chase surpassing Chevy.

Into Boston marched their forces, musket-barrels brightly gleaming,
Colors flying, sabres flashing, drums were beating, fifes were screaming.
Not a word about their journey ; from the general to the drummer,
Did you ask about their doings, than a statue each was dumber ;
But the wounded in their litters, lying pallid, weak, and gory,
With a language clear and certain told the sanguinary story.

'Twas a dark and bloody lesson ; it was bloody work to teach it ;
But when sits on high Oppression, soaring fire alone can reach it.
Though but raw and rude Provincials, we were freemen, and contending
For the rights our fathers gave us, and a country worth defending ;
And when foul invaders threaten wrong to hearthstone and to altar,
Shame were on the freeman's manhood should he either fail or falter.

On the day the fight that followed, neighbor met and talked with neigh-
    bor ;
First the few who fell they buried, then returned to daily labor.
Glowed the fire within the forges, ran the ploughshare down the furrow,
Clicked the bobbin-loaded shuttle—both our fight and toil were thorough ;
If we labored in the battle, or the shop, or forge, or fallow,
Still there came an honest purpose, casting round our deeds a halo.

Though they strove again, these minions of Germaine and North and
    Gower,
They could never make the weakest of our band before them cower ;

Neither England's bribes nor soldiers, force of arms nor titles splendid,
Could deprive of what our fathers left as rights to be defended.
And the flame from Concord, spreading, kindled kindred conflagrations,
Till the Colonies United took their place among the nations.

MONUMENT AT CONCORD.

THE Provincial Congress of South Carolina, in 1775, appointed a Committee of Safety to sit during its own recess, and to this it delegated full power. The Committee fitted out a vessel, which captured an English sloop, laden with powder, lying at St. Augustine. The royal governor of the State sent couriers to intercept the vessel, but they failed. The powder was brought to Charleston, and part of it was used by Arnold in the siege of Quebec. Later in the year Colonel Moultrie took possession of a small fort standing on Sullivan's Island, in Charleston Harbor. The governor fled to the frigate *Tamar*, and the Committee of Safety took charge of affairs. Fort John-

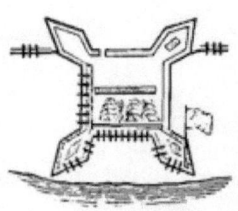

PLAN OF FORT ON SULLI-
VAN'S ISLAND.

WILLIAM MOULTRIE.

son, on James's Island, was seized and armed. Guns were mounted on Haddrell's Point, and a fascine battery made on Sullivan's Island. Between these two the *Tamar* and her consort were obliged to leave the harbor. Colonel Moultrie was now ordered to build a strong fort on Sullivan's Island, and over three hundred guns were mounted on the various fortifications. Colonel Gadsden was placed in command, and every preparation made for a vigorous defence.

The Continental Congress knew that a combined naval and land attack would be made on Charleston; and in April Brigadier-general Armstrong was sent there to take command, but was superseded, on the fourth of June, by Major-general Charles Lee, who had been sent by Washington. He worked hard for the defence of the city, and was supported with ardor and enthusiasm by the people. Troops flocked

SOUTH CAROLINA
FLAG.

SULLIVAN'S ISLAND, AND THE BRITISH FLEET
AT THE TIME OF THE ATTACK.

in until there were between five and six thousand men in arms, including the Northern troops that had come with Armstrong and Lee. They were disposed at Fort Johnson, on James's Island, under Gadsden ; a battery on Sullivan's Island, under Thomson ; in the fort on the same island, under Moultrie ; and at Haddrell's Point, under Lee.

The British arrived on the fourth of June, but it was not until the twenty-eighth that they were ready to attack. During the interval they had constructed batteries on Long Island, to silence that of Thomson on Sullivan's Island and cover the landing of the storming-party of Clinton's troops.

On the morning of the twenty-eighth of June the attack began. The incidents are faithfully given in the ballad, and to that the reader is referred.

SULLIVAN'S ISLAND.

Stout Sir Henry Clinton spoke—
" It is time the power awoke
   That upholds in these dominions
      Royal right ;
Set all sail, and southward steer,
And, instead of idling here,   .
   Crush these rebel Carolinians
      Who have dared to beard our might."

Of his coming well we knew—
Far and wide the story flew,
   And the many tongues of rumor
      Swelled his force ;
But we scorned his gathered might,
And, relying on the right,
   Bade the braggart let his humor
      For a battle take its course.

Neither idle nor dismayed,
As we watched the coming shade
   Of the murky cloud that hovered
      On our coast ;
From the country far and near,
In we called the volunteer,
   Till the ground around was covered
      With the trampling of our host.

In their homespun garb arrayed,
Sturdy farmers to our aid
   Came, as to a bridal lightly
      Come the guests ;

4

Leaving crops and kine and lands,
Trusty weapons in their hands,
   And the fire of courage brightly
      Burning in their manly breasts.

SIR HENRY CLINTON.

[From an English Print.]

From the hills the hunters came—
Having dealt with meaner game,
   Much they longed to meet the lions
      Of the isles ;
And 'twas pleasant there to see
With what stately step, and free,
   Strode those restless-eyed Orions
      Past our better-ordered files.

There were soldiers from the North,
Hailed as brothers by the swarth,
   Keen, chivalric Carolinians
      At their side—
Ah, may never discord's fires,
   Sons of heart-united sires

Who together fought the minions
  Of a tyrant-king, divide !

Came the owner of the soil,
The mechanic from his toil,
  And the student from the college—
      Equal each ;
They had gathered there to show
To the proud and cruel foe,
  Who had come to court the knowledge,
    What a people's wrath could teach.

Watching Clinton, day by day,
From his vessels in the bay,
  On Long Island beach debarking
      Grenadiers,
In the fort at Sullivan's isle,
With a grim and meaning smile,
  Every scarlet soldier marking,
    Stood our ready cannoneers.

Of palmetto logs and sand,
On a stretch of barren land,
  Stands that rude but strong obstruction,
      Keeping guard ;
'Tis the shelter of the town—
They must take or break it down,
  They must sweep it to destruction,
    Or their farther path is barred.

'Twas but weak they thought to shield ;
They were sure it soon would yield ;
  They had guns afloat before it,
      Ten to one ;
Yet long time their vessels lay
Idly rocking in the bay,
  While the flag that floated o'er it
    Spread its colors in the sun.

But at length toward the noon
Of the twenty-eighth of June,

We observed their force in motion
On the shore ;
At the hour of half-past nine
Saw their frigates form in line,
Heard the krakens of the ocean
Ope their mighty jaws and roar.

On the decks we saw them stand,
Lighted matches held in hand,
Brawny sailors, stripped and ready
For the word ;
Crawling to the royal's head,
Saw the signal rise and spread ;
And the order to be steady
To the waiting crews we heard.

Then the iron balls and fire,
From the lips of cannon dire,
In a blazing torrent pouring,
Roaring came ;
And each dun and rolling cloud
That arose the ships to shroud,
Seemed a mist continual soaring
From some cataract of flame.

Moultrie eyed the *Bristol* then—
She was foremost of the ten—
And these words, his eyes upon her,
Left his lips :
"Let them not esteem you boors ;
Show that gentle blood of yours ;
Pay the Admiral due honor,
And the line-of-battle ships."

Back our balls in answer flew,
Piercing plank and timbers through,
Till the foe began to wonder
At our might ;
While we laughed to hear the roar
Flung by Echo from the shore ;

While we shouted to the thunder
  Grandly pealing through the fight.

From Long Island Clinton came,
To surmount the wall of flame
  That was built by Thomson's rangers
      On the east ;
But he found a banquet spread
Where, with open hand and red,
  Dangers bade the hostile strangers
      Bloody welcome to the feast.

Moved their boats, with soldiers filled,
Rowed by seamen picked and skilled,
  O'er the channel, urging proudly
      To attack ;
Stern and silently they moved,
As became their courage proved,
  Though the rangers' rifles, loudly
      Speaking peril, warned them back.

Long the barges headway held,
By the sinewy arms impelled
  Of the dauntless British seamen,
      Through the foam ;
Through the leaden death that came,
Borne upon the wings of flame,
  From the rifled guns of freemen
      Fighting fiercely for their home.

One by one the rowers dropped ;
Then their onward course was stopped—
  Death stood ready for the daring
      At the oar ;
Though in scorn they came at first,
When the storm upon them burst
  They returned with humbler bearing
      To the safe and farther shore.

Then the bluff Sir Peter cried,
"Though they lower Clinton's pride,
      4*

And with front as stern as iron
   Are arrayed,
There's a joint within their mail—
To their western front shall sail
  The *Actæon*, *Sphynx*, and *Siren*,
  And the fortress enfilade."

SIR PETER PARKER.

Oh, the admiral was too free
With his gallant frigates three!
  It were better had he kept them
    As they were;
For the Middle Shoal they found,
Where they snugly lay aground,
  While so bloodily we swept them
    With our iron besoms there.

They were taught full soon aright
That the bravest man in flight
  May, when perils dire environ,
    Safety find:
Soon, by aid of sail and sweep,
From the shoal unto the deep

MOULTRIE MONUMENT, WITH JASPER'S STATUE.

They restored the *Sphynx* and *Siren*,
  But the other stayed behind.

Gnawed the admiral his lip ;
Yet the combat from his ship
  Coolly, 'mid our fire so deadly,
    Guided he,
Though the dying and the dead
On the decks around were spread,
  And the blood was running redly
    From the scuppers to the sea.

On that bloody deck he stood,
While, with voices deep and rude,
  Thrice a hundred cannons thundered
    For the King ;
And our thirty cannon black
Growled their terrible answer back,
  Till the souls from bodies sundered
    Of three hundred men took wing.

All the while the battle through
Waved our crescent flag of blue,
  Till the staff was cut asunder
    By a ball ;
And the foemen raised a cheer,
Like the crow of chanticleer,
  Shrilly sounding through the thunder
    As they saw the color fall.

On the ramparts Jasper stood,
In his hands that banner good,
  'Mid the balls that flew incessant
    O'er the brine ;
To a sponge-staff firmly tied
Once again it floated wide,
  Flashing to the sun the crescent
    Of the Carolina line.

Rang the stirring cheer on cheer
For our hero void of fear,

For our young and gallant sergeant
    Firm and bold ;
And we swore our bones should bleach
On that barren, sandy beach,
    Ere that flag with crescent argent
        Should be wrested from our hold.

So we fought till set of sun,
When their vessels, one by one,
    Slackened fire, and, anchor weighing,
        Shaped a course ;
To Five Fathom Hole they fled
With their dying and their dead,
    In their battered hulls displaying
        How our skill surpassed their force.

Through the night we never slept—
Ceaseless watch and ward we kept,
    With the port-fire steady burning
        At each gun ;
And the vessels of our foes
We beheld when dawn arose—
    Eastwardly our glances turning—
        Lie between us and the sun.

Yet not all escaped that day :
The *Actæon* frigate lay
    At the shoal whereon she grounded
        Hours before ;
And her vexed and angry crew,
As our shot at her we threw,
    And her sides of oak we pounded,
        Left the guns and took the oar.

We beheld them from the deck
Of her rent and tattered wreck,
    Like the rats from garner burning,
        Fastly flee ;
Ah, no more before the gale
Will that gallant vessel sail ;
    Nevermore, the billows spurning,
        Wave her white wings o'er the sea !

Ere they fled, with spiteful ire
They devoted her to fire,
  With her red-cross ensign proudly
      Floating free;
But we boarded with a crew,
Down the flying colors drew,
  While our cheers rang long and loudly
    To the fortress from the sea.

CHARLESTON IN 1780.

Then her small-arms all we took,
And her bell and signal-book;
  Fired her cannon thrice, in honor
      Of the day;
Bore her colors ensign down,
In defiance of the crown;
  And to heap more scorn upon her,
    Jeering, trailed them o'er the bay.

Then we fired her as before,
And, exulting, from the shore
  Saw the flaming serpents creeping
    Up the shrouds;
Saw them dance upon the deck,
Saw them lick and gnaw the wreck,
  Saw them to the mast-heads leaping
    Through the rolling, smoking clouds.

Then, while gleamed the sparks like stars,
Snapped and fell the blazing spars,
  While the fire was moaning dirges,
    Came a roar;
Upward sprang a pillared flame,
And to fragments rent her frame,
  With a shock that drove the surges,
    White with terror, to the shore.

Time since then has travelled on:
Moultrie, Thomson, Jasper, gone!
  Few survive who shared the glory
    Of the scene;
But their names in light shall blaze
To the very latter days,
  And our sons, in song and story,
    Keep their memory ever green.

DURING the latter part of 1776, affairs looked gloomy for the new Confederacy of the States. The affair at White Plains, the fall of Fort Washington, and the evacuation of Fort Lee, followed by the retreat across New Jersey, had reduced the forces of Washington to less than three thousand men. The enemy occupied Newark, New Brunswick, Princeton, Trenton, and

Bordentown. They were thus scattered in detachments on a long line. When Washington crossed the river Delaware—which he did after securing every available boat on the shore—his force had dwindled to twenty-two hundred men; and this number was still further reduced by the expiration of the term of enlistment of a large portion. Congress had fled to Baltimore, and Cornwallis was about to seize Philadelphia.

Congress now ordered increased pay to the troops, with liberal bounties, and by inde-
fatigable exertions the ranks began to fill again. On the twenty-fourth of December, Washington's army amounted to over ten thousand men, of which about half were effective. With these
he determined to make a simultaneous attack upon the detached British posts on the New
Jersey side. The main force, led by Washington in person, was to cross at M'Conkey's Ferry,
and fall upon the Hessians, under Rahl, at Trenton. Cadwallader was to cross near Bristol,
and Ewing below Trenton Falls, to attack Mount Holly, Black Horse, Bordentown, and Burling-
ton. He was aided unexpectedly by General Putnam, who commanded at Philadelphia. Learning of the design to attack Trenton, Putnam sent a small body of militia, under Colonel Griffin,
to Mount Holly, where he was not to fight, but to retreat before the enemy. Count Donop,

RAHL'S HEAD-QUARTERS.

at Bordentown, fell into the trap, followed
Griffin, and was not at hand to support
Rahl at the critical moment. Neither Ewing nor Cadwallader could effect a crossing. The latter got a battalion of foot over
the river, but not being able to cross the
artillery, these had to return.

The incidents of the surprise are correctly given in the ballad. The loss of the
Americans was only four — two frozen to
death and two killed in battle. The loss
of the Hessians amounted to six officers
and over twenty men killed, and twenty-
three officers and eight hundred and eighty-
six privates made prisoners. Six brass

field-pieces, four colors, and a thousand stand of arms were also taken.

The effect of this movement was inspiriting, and gave great hope and encouragement to
the Americans. The English commander, who had thought the war was at an end, now
learned that his task had begun again. Numbers of Americans whose term of service had
expired re-enlisted, and the militia were eager to turn out whenever their services were
demanded.

THE SURPRISE AT TRENTON.

SCENE.—A Pennsylvania farm-house on the Delaware.   TIME.—December 25, 1836.
REUBEN COMFORT *loquitur*.

Ruth, help Friend English to a chair. Thee's welcome. Thee would know
The ferry where they crossed the stream, now sixty years ago,
To take the Hessians under Rahl? There's nothing now to see.
There had been that to stir thee much, had thee been there with me:
For I, though but a stripling then, trained ever to abhor
All force and strife, that raging flood crossed with the men of war.

Thee stares! Thee doubtless wonders much a Friend should have to say
That his communication had been more than yea or nay;
That he had been in battle where his fellow-men were slain,
And, favored to escape all harm, came back in peace again.
'Twas very wrong to violate peace principles of Friends.
Well, well! The Meeting dealt with me, and there the matter ends.

Tell thee about it? Yes, although 'twas little of a fight.
Abner, thee put up this friend's beast; he'll tarry here to-night.
And thee must take into thee mind, those who in battle stand
Know little of what's going on, save just on either hand;
And much of my recital thee will find much better told
In some well-written chronicle made in the days of old.

BATTLE OF TRENTON.

But I could tell thee all about the crossing ere the day,
The marching up to Birmingham, the silence by the way,
The rushing into Trenton with friend Sullivan and those;
And how when first we saw the foe a mighty shouting rose;
And I can tell thee something more which no one else could do—
Can name to thee the very man who Rahl the Hessian slew.

Thee knows where Newbold's Island stands? Thee ought. Yes, that is
      true;
The English Farm has nigh it stood since sixteen-eighty-two.
Thee knows the old stone farm-house looking out upon the tide
Slantwise across the river on the Pennsylvany side?

In that house I was born and bred, and lived till twenty-one,
As all the Comforts had for years, from father unto son.

That year my father rode up here and bought this farm for me;
For Issachar he lived at home, and we could not agree.
He leaned too much on his birthright, so father to us said,
"Two farms had better hold ye!" and he got me this instead;
And I came here to work it. 'Twas a goodly start in life:
The place had been well tilled, and all I needed was a wife.

I went among the women-folk, as usual with a youth,
And soon I fell in love with one, Friend Scudder's daughter, Ruth;
And straightway found the damsel moved, and in her spirit free
Before the Friends in meeting to stand up along with me.
And we would be united, if our people's minds were clear,
On Fourth-day of the first week of the First-month in next year.

The weeks that came were pleasant weeks, the world was all in tune;
The stars were always bright at night, the month was fair as June.
Dear Ruth! whose eyes were mild as doves', whose tones were sweet as
    birds'—
More pleasant was the maid to me than gold or land or herds.
Sweet Ruth! at eighty-two my ears find music in the name;
But human bliss must reach its end, and bleak December came.

Meanwhile the people round us fought, the country was one camp;
Sometimes, far in the dead of night, I'd hear the soldiers' tramp.
The Friends were loyal? Nay, not all; if loyalty be such
As favors fraud and winks at wrong, then few were loyal—much;
Yet few felt free to go to war—they dwelt upon the word
Which says that they who take the sword shall perish by the sword.

It was a chilly morning when, foreboding naught of harm,
I crossed the river in my skiff, and sought the Scudder farm:
About the hour when Ruth would have her household work all through,
And ready be to take a walk, the scene around to view.
The trees were leafless, and the ground was covered half with snow;
But what is that to human hearts with youth and love aglow!

We wandered up and down the road like children, hand in hand,
And talked about the future, and the life before us planned;

But while we spake the sound of hoofs upon the ground we heard—
Somehow my spirit to its depth by that same sound was stirred;
And closer Ruth towards me drew that slender form of hers,
As came the clanking of a sword whose scabbard clinked with spurs.

We turned. A horseman was at hand, in gay apparel clad,
Upon his dark-green coat much braid and golden lace he had;
A man of goodly presence. He gazed curiously at each,
Then spake (thee knows we understand round here the German speech):
"Ah! Sie ist deine Schwester, Mann?"—at which I shook my head.
"So! deine Frau vielleicht? 'ne Braut! Sehr gut! Ein Schmatz!" he
    said.

"There, that will do, friend officer," in wrath was my reply;
"I feel not free, when thus thee speaks, to stand in silence by.
Pray go thy ways; we're peaceful folk, nor meddle thee nor thine."
"Dat's zafe," he said, "in dimes like dese; gleichwohl der Kuss ist
    mein!"
With that he bent to where she stood; but ere her lips he found,
I dragged him headlong from his horse, and hurled him to the ground.

He rose, and straightway drew his sword, and angrily he glared;
I thought my hour of death had come when he his weapon bared.
The veins upon his forehead swelled, and then his face grew white;
With rage that gave him double strength he raised the blade to smite.
And as it rose I heard a scream; Ruth rushed between us twain;
Fell terribly the keen-edged steel: my pretty dove was slain.

He shrank in horror; from his face all trace of color fled,
While I sank down upon my knees beside the pulseless dead;
And loud I cried, "A deed is thine which even fiends abhor!
Her soul shall rise and thine shall sink, thou bloody wolf of war!"
"Ach Gott!" he said, and spake no more; then, mounting on his steed,
Struck deep the rowels in its flanks, and rode in headlong speed.

Ruth did not on the instant die, and, ere she breathed her last,
Soft cradled in my loving arms, her life-blood flowing fast,
There went a shudder through her frame, a glazing of the eye,
And then a lighting of her face, a glance at earth and sky.
So tenderly she murmured, with a loving look to me,
"Reuben! 'tis hard in youth to die, but sweet to die for thee?"

5

We placed her in Friends' burying-ground; and, though we marked it not,
I could take thee to it in the night, so well I know the spot.
At home for many hours I lay—a stupor on me came;
The only sound that roused me up was mention of her name.
And then Friend Scudder and his wife, who stood beside me, said,
"Who does his living duty pays most honor to the dead."

Three weeks had passed; it was the night at close of Christmas-day—
So the world's people name it—when, in all of war's array,
But silently and cautiously, a force at nightfall came
And seized what few bateaux there were; they took my skiff the same.
And then I knew the wrath of God was gathering round to fall
Upon the hireling Hessian force, and its commander, Rahl.

The spirit moved within me then; I sought out him who led
The soldiers in the battle, and thus to the man I said,
"Friend Washington, although thee knows that Friends are men of peace,
Who pray continual night and day this bloody strife may cease,
Yet it is given unto me that I should go this night
And cross the stream with these thy friends to guide their steps aright."

The general looked at me well pleased. "You meet us in our need;
The way is plain, but such a night our footsteps might mislead.
Get him a musket, Baylor." But I quickly answered "Nay!
The carnal weapon suits me not; I have a better stay.
Unarmed I go before thy men when once the stream be crossed,
And, though the air be black with storm, our path shall not be lost."

They then embarked the soldiers, 'mid the blinding snow and hail;
They struggled with the driven ice, the current, and the gale;
And much I marvelled, as I gazed upon the piteous sight,
What men endure when in a cause that they consider right;
For nearly all were poorly clad to meet the biting air:
Some were half naked in the ranks, and some with feet all bare.

And back and forth the boats were sent upon the watery way,
So long that when we all had crossed the sky was tinged with grey.
Right on we marched to Birmingham, a moment there made stand,
Then broke in two divisions which filed off on either hand.
One half, with Washington and Greene, the old Scotch highway chose;
The other took the river road—I went ahead of those.

Before we parted, some one came and said to Washington,
"The priming in the guns is wet; what now is to be done?"
"Then let them use the bayonet!" was his answer to the man;
At which a hum of confidence among the soldiers ran.
All filled with silent, stern resolve, they strode so proudly then,
I knew they would before the foe acquit themselves like men.

The sun arose, and still we marched, I somewhat in advance,
A voice cried, "Wer da? Halt!" I saw a musket-barrel glance.
"A friend," I answered. "Freund von wem?" "A friend to Washington!"
The sentry fired and missed, and ran and cast away his gun;
For now behind me, pressing on, he saw our troops were near,
And in the distance on our left I heard Greene's forces cheer.

"Move faster there!" cried Sullivan, "or Greene will get ahead.
Press on and use your steel, my men; we have no need of lead."
And on they rushed, I with the rest; through Water Street we swept,
While from a few upon our front some scattered bullets leapt.
Their outguard fled in sore affright, and one there dying lay,
His loaded musket by his side—his work was done that day.

I saw the Hessian soldiers that were forming into rank;
I saw their mounted officers—could hear the scabbards clank,
As hither, thither, riding round, they drove their men in line;
And through them all, from each to each, went eager glance of mine,
Till in their very centre there I saw one on his horse,
His orders coolly giving, the commander of their force.

I knew him! I could not forget! 'Twas he whose angry blow
Had smote my darling to the death; he should not 'scape me so.
I cast my plain coat to the ground. "Quaker, lie there!" said I.
"Yon is the son of Amalek! I'll smite him hip and thigh!"
And from the ground that musket caught, and o'er its barrel drew
A bead as fine as a needle's point: the ball his breast went through.

The musket dropped from out my hands—a fellow man I'd slain;
My heart stood still, but presently I was myself again.
I leaned against a tree. A sound of cannon smote my ear,
A rattling fire of musketry, then silence, then a cheer.
I knew they had surrendered. Well, what if the place were won?
I turned and wandered to my home; my errand had been done.

When Friends would have disowned me as a man of blood and sin,
Friend Scudder spake—you might have heard the falling of a pin—
"God knows His own wise purposes; who'd scan His ways must fail.
Who gave the Israelitish dame the hammer and the nail,
His wrath has fallen on bloody Rahl, on Sisera laid low;
And Reuben Comfort did God's work.   In peace then let him go."

Loud weeping on the women's side, and sobs on ours that day;
And no one there gainsaid his words, and no one uttered nay.
The brethren came and pressed my hand before I left the place,
And all the women, as I passed, looked pitying in my face.
So I went forth of man forgiven.   I pray that God may be,
When sitting in the latter day, as merciful to me.

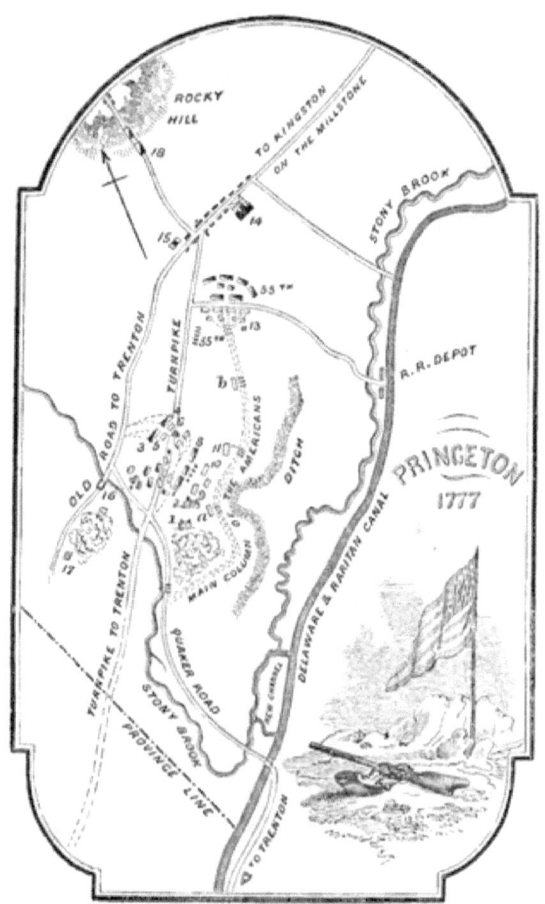

SUBSEQUENT OPERATIONS.

FOLLOWING THE OPERATIONS AT TRENTON.

AFTER the capture of the Hessians at Trenton, the American army, under the influence of enthusiasm and a bounty of ten dollars, hard money, to each recruit, filled up rapidly. Washington determined to re-occupy Trenton and make it the basis of offensive operations. He re-crossed the river on the 30th of December, and soon learned of the approach of Cornwallis with a large force. The number of each army was the same; but the British were all well-trained regulars, while the greater part of the Americans was made up of raw militia-men. Washington moved to some high ground on the north side of the Assunpink, and guarded the bridge spanning the stream. A strong party, under General Greene, had so harassed the enemy that he did not reach Trenton until evening. He had driven Greene so close that he got over the bridge with difficulty. There was a ford above, but this and the bridge were covered by field-pieces. The British attempted to force the bridge, but were three times repulsed with loss; and a similar attempt at the ford met with like results. The action was kept up with cannon and musketry until after dark, when it ceased, and both parties lit their camp-fires, and prepared to renew hostilities in the morning.

FRIENDS' MEETING-HOUSE.

Cornwallis, confident that Washington could not escape, rested content. His antagonist knew the inferiority of his troops and the probable disastrous consequences of a general engagement. To avoid this, at a council of war it was suggested to march off at night down the river, and cross to Philadelphia. Washington preferred to move upon Princeton, where a body of British troops were stationed, and if possible reach New Brunswick and destroy the enemy's stores. There was one difficulty in the way: it was impossible to move forty pieces of artillery over the surrounding swamp. At that juncture it began to grow intensely cold, and in two hours the marshy ground was frozen hard. The army moved in silence, leaving camp-fires burning, and a small party to make a feint of intrenching. The British were completely deceived. At morning the camp-fires were still blazing, but the Americans had disappeared. While they were endeavoring to find out what route Washington had taken, they heard the booming of cannon at Princeton.

The Americans took what is known as the Quaker road, which was new and full of stumps of trees. These impeded their progress so much that it was about sunrise before they reached the upper bridge over Stony Brook, near Princeton, and formed in column near Friends' Meeting-house. Here they came on a brigade of the enemy, under Mawhood, two regiments of which were on their way to join Cornwallis. The latter discovered the Americans, who now emerged from the

VIEW OF THE BATTLE-GROUND NEAR PRINCETON.

woods south of the meeting-house. Mawhood by a quick movement brought two of his regiments to the bridge at Worth's Mills, and crossed just as Mercer, who had been detached there with a small party, reached it. Both parties tried to get possession of the high grounds. Mercer reached Clark's orchard, and finding the enemy approaching from the heights, sheltered his riflemen behind a hedge, from which they poured a destructive fire. The enemy returned the fire and charged, driving the Americans with the bayonet. They pursued, and when they came to the brow of the heights, discovered the American force, under Washington, approaching. The fugitives were re-formed, and a battery, under Moulder, began to play on Mawhood's men. An attempt to take this failed, and Mawhood, seeing a Connecticut regiment advancing, retreated, leaving his artillery. It was during this affair that General Mercer received his death-wound.

The broken British managed to escape and joined Cornwallis, now on the advance. The Americans, pushing on to Princeton, met the 55th regiment, which they routed, and that and the 40th fled to New Brunswick. A few companies remained in the college, but these, under a cannonade, surrendered. The bridge over Stony Brook was now destroyed, just as the van of the British appeared. They forded the stream, but when at the town were brought up by a single discharge from a 32-pounder which the British had before left on a temporary breastwork. This gave them the idea that the Americans intended to make a stand, and they prepared for battle. After some delay they threw out reconnoitring parties, and felt their way cautiously, to discover that Washington was far away on the road to Millstone with his prisoners and spoils. He destroyed the bridge at Kingston, and filed off to the left, arriving at Pluckemin that night. Cornwallis, after repairing the bridge, supposed Washington had gone to New Brunswick, and pushed on in that direction, to be disappointed.

ASSUNPINK AND PRINCETON.

Glorious the day when in arms at Assunpink,
    And after at Princeton the Briton we met;
Few in both armies—they'd skirmishes call them,
    Now hundreds of thousands in battle are set.
But for the numbers engaged, let me tell you,
    Smart brushes they were, and two battles that told;
There 'twas I first drew a bead on a foeman—
    I, a mere stripling, not twenty years old.

Tell it? Well, friends, that is just my intention;
    There's nothing a veteran hates and abhors
More than a chance lost to tell his adventures,
    Or give you his story of battles and wars.
Nor is it wonder old men are loquacious,
    And talk, if you listen, from sun unto sun;
Youth has the power to be up and be doing,
    While age can but tell of the deeds it has done.

Ranged for a mile on the banks of Assunpink,
    There, southward of Trenton, one morning we lay,
When, with his red-coats all marshalled to meet us,
    Cornwallis came fiercely at close of the day—

Driving some scouts who had gone out with Longstreet,
   From where they were crossing at Shabbaconk Run—
Trumpets loud blaring, drums beating, flags flying—
   Three hours, by the clock, before setting of sun.

Two ways were left them by which to assail us,
   And neither was perfectly to their desire—
One was the bridge we controlled by our cannon,
   The other the ford that was under our fire.
"Death upon one side, and Dismal on t'other,"
   Said Sambo, our cook, as he gazed on our foes:
Cheering and dauntless they marched to the battle,
   And, doubtful of choice, both the dangers they chose.

Down at the ford, it was said, that the water
   Was reddened with blood from the soldiers who fell:
As for the bridge, where they tried it, their forces
   Were beaten with terrible slaughter, as well.
Grape-shot swept causeway, and pattered on water,
   And riddled their columns, that broke and gave way;
Thrice they charged boldly, and thrice they retreated;
   Then darkness came down, and so ended the fray.

How did I get there? I came from our corn-mill
   At noon of the day when the battle begun,
Bringing in flour to the troops under Proctor;
   'Twas not very long ere that errand was done.
Up to that time I had never enlisted,
   Though Jacob, my brother, had entered with Wayne;
But the fight stirred me; I sent back the horses,
   And made up my mind with the rest to remain.

We camped on *our* side—the south—of Assunpink,
   While *they* bivouacked for the night upon *theirs*;
Both posting sentries and building up watchfires,
   With those on both sides talking over affairs.
"Washington's caught in a trap!" said Cornwallis,
   And smiled with a smile that was joyous and grim;
"Fox! but I have him!"—the earl had mistaken;
   The fox, by the coming of daylight, had him.

Early that night, when the leaders held council,
  Both St. Clair and Reed said our action was clear ;
Useless to strike at the van of our foemen—
  His force was too strong ; we must fall on his rear.
Washington thought so, and bade us replenish
  Our watchfires till nearly the dawn of the day ;
Setting some more to make feint of intrenching,
  While swiftly in darkness the rest moved away.

Marching by Sandtown, and Quaker Bridge crossing,
  We passed Stony Creek a full hour before dawn,
Leaving there Mercer with one scant battalion
  Our foes to amuse, should they find we were gone ;
Then the main force pushed its way into Princeton,
  All ready to strike those who dreamed of no blow ;
Only a chance that we lost not our labor,
  And slipped through our fingers, unknowing, the foe.

Mawhood's brigade, never feeling its danger,
  Had started for Trenton at dawn of the day,
Crossèd Stony Creek, after we had gone over,
  When Mercer's weak force they beheld on its way ;
Turning contemptuously back to attack it,
  They drove it with ease in disorder ahead—
Firelocks alone were no match for their cannon—
  A fight, and then flight, and brave Mercer lay dead.

Murdered, some said, while imploring for quarter—
  A dastardly deed, if the thing had been true—
Cruel our foes, but in that thing we wronged them,
  And let us in all give the demon his due.
Gallant Hugh Mercer fell sturdily fighting,
  So long as his right arm his sabre could wield,
Stretching his enemies bleeding around him,
  And then, overpowered, fell prone on the field.

Hearing the firing, we turned and we met them,
  Our cannon replying to theirs with a will ;
Fiercely with grape and with canister swept them,
  And chased them in wrath from the brow of the hill.

Racing and chasing it was into Princeton,
  Where, seeking the lore to be taught in that hall,
Red-coats by scores entered college, but stayed not—
  We rudely expelled them with powder and ball.

BATTLE OF PRINCETON.

Only a skirmish, you see, though a sharp one—
  It did not last over the fourth of an hour;
But 'twas a battle that did us this service—
  No more, from that day, had we fear of their power.
Trenton revived us, Assunpink encouraged,
  But Princeton gave hope that we held to the last;
Flood-tide had come on the black, sullen water,
  And ebb-tide for ever and ever had passed.

Yes! 'twas the turn of the tide in our favor—
  A turn of the tide to a haven that bore.
Had Lord Cornwallis crossed over Assunpink
  That day we repelled him, our fighting were o'er.
Had he o'ertaken us ere we smote Mawhood,
  All torn as we were, it seems certain to me,
I would not chatter to you about battles,
  And you and your children would not have been free.

DONALD M'DONALD.

THE affair on which this lyric is founded is entirely different from the attack on the fort at Schoharie by Johnson and Brant. It was a raid by a party of loyalists and Indians, led by a Tory partisan, Donald M'Donald. He was an active and relentless leader; but not so bloody as Walter Butler. He should not be confounded with the loyalist general of the same name in North Carolina. He commanded part of the loyalists in the fight near Conewawah during Sullivan's expedition.

M'Donald died from wounds received in a very singular conflict. A German, named Schell —the name usually spelled Shell—had founded a little settlement about five miles north of Herkimer, which was known as Shell's Bush. Here he built a block-house, the upper story projecting all around. One August afternoon, while the people were at work out-of-doors, M'Donald, with sixty men, made a descent on the Bush. The inhabitants generally fled to Fort Dayton. Schell saw the enemy almost too late, but managed to escape to the block-house, with two of his sons—two others were taken. With the aid of Mrs. Schell, who loaded the guns, the little garrison made a vigorous defence. M'Donald, failing in an attempt to burn the block-house, tried to open the door with a crow-bar. A shot from Schell wounded him in the leg, and he was unable to stand. Schell opened the door, dragged in M'Donald, and closed it. Then he stripped his prisoner of all the cartridges he had. Schell felt he had an insurance against fire while his prisoner was inside. But the enemy, enraged at the loss of some of their number, made a rush to the house, and five of them put the ends of their pieces through the loop-holes. Mrs. Schell bent the barrels with the blows of an axe, and Schell and his sons fired down on them. At dusk Schell called to his wife from the second story, and told her that Captain Small was coming from Fort Dayton. Presently he gave directions loudly to imaginary troops, and the enemy taking fright ran away. M'Donald's leg was taken off next day at Fort Dayton, but he died soon after the operation.

COLONEL HARPER'S CHARGE.

As eastward the shadows were steadily creeping,
Fair wives were at spinning, stout husbands at reaping.

Loud chattered the children with no one to hush them;
None knew that the thunder was stooping to crush them.

But soon from the forest, the hill, and the dingle,
Came footmen and horsemen, in bodies and single.

Wild, painted Cayugas, relentless and fearless,
More barbarous Tories, black-hearted and tearless.

To hearth-stone and roof-tree destruction to carry,
The cruel M'Donald came down on Schoharie.

No mercy was offered, no quarter was given;
The souls of the victims departed unshriven.

Their requiem only the shrieks of the flying,
The yells of the slayers, the groans of the dying.

Too weak in our numbers to venture a sally,
We sat in our fortress and looked on the valley.

We heard the wild uproar, the screaming and yelling,
The firing and crashing, of butchery telling.

No tiger imprisoned in iron-bound caging
Felt half of our fury or equalled our raging.

Yet what could we hinder? Revenge was denied us,
While ten times our number to battle defied us.

Though wild was our anguish and deep our despairing,
With three hundred to fight would be imbecile daring.

But Colonel John Harper, who chafed at the ravage,
The pillage and murder, by Tory and savage,

Urged us on to the combat, and angrily showered
Hot words on our chief as a cold-blooded coward.

We heard all his raving of anger in sadness;
We never resented, but pitied his madness.

John Harper looked round him, and said he scorned favor,
He'd seek for assistance from men who were braver.

He called for his horse, and defied us to stay him,
And scoffed at the cowards who dared not obey him.

His foot in the stirrups, he hearkened to no man,
Sank spurs to their rowels, and charged through the foeman.

He scattered them fiercely, and, ere they could rally,
Away like an arrow he shot through the valley.

He broke through the circle created to bound him;
The bullets they showered fell harmlessly round him.

When fair in the saddle, he never was idle;
He rode through the darkness, and kept a loose bridle.

On, on through the darkness, till daylight was o'er him,
And Albany's houses rose proudly before him.

We heard the shots rattle, we saw his foes rally,
And thought that his life-blood had moistened the valley.

Meanwhile in the fortress, through all the night dreary,
We watched till the sunrise, disheartened and weary.

Noon came in its splendor; we saw them preparing
To storm our rude ramparts, and laughed at their daring.

For we were in shelter, and they were uncovered—
There was work for the buzzards that over us hovered.

Each step they took forward, with eagerness timing,
We handled our rifles, and looked to the priming.

But, stay! is this real, or only delusion?
What means their blank terror, their sudden confusion?

The whole of the foemen seem stricken with one dread—
'Tis Colonel John Harper, with horsemen a hundred!

We gaze but a moment in rapture and wonder—
Rides Harper like lightning, we fall like the thunder.

To saddle, M'Donald! your doom has been spoken;
The tigers are on you, the bars have been broken.

Whose horse is the swiftest may ride from the foray;
No hope for the footman if savage or Tory.

The heart shuts on pity when vengeance is portress;
And husbands and fathers came forth from the fortress.

As the wails of our wives and our babes we remember,
The bright fire of mercy goes out—the last ember.

They meant but a visit, we forced them to tarry;
But few of the foemen went back from Schoharie.

THE BATTLE-GROUND OF ORISKANY.

ORISKANY.

THE battle at Oriskany is one of the many instances during the Revolutionary contest where disaster resulted through the rashness and insubordination of inferior officers. A lack of discipline continually placed the cause in peril, and success was frequently won at a cost which might have been avoided. The enemy, under the command of Johnson and Brant, were, fortunately for their antagonists, troubled with the same fault. Had it been otherwise, the Americans would have been exterminated.

PETER GANSEVOORT.

The enemy had laid siege to Fort Schuyler, where Gansevoort lay with a small garrison. General Herkimer, though without much pretensions to military science, was a brave and prudent officer, and perfectly fitted for the occasion. He had called out the militia of Tryon County to the number of eight hundred. His plan was to make an attack upon the enemy simultaneously with a sortie from the fort, and he sent a messenger to effect that arrangement with Gansevoort. The signal for Herkimer's advance was to be a single gun from Fort Schuyler. It was some time before the scout could make his way safely through the investing force. In the mean while some of the men grew impatient, and clamored for an immediate advance. Colonels Cox and Paris headed this party, and when Herkimer refused they denounced him as a coward. At length he submitted to a precipitous movement, at the same time saying that these very bold gentlemen would be the first to run. And so it proved.

The incidents of the fight are so minutely given in the ballad that no further explanation is needed. The Americans remained masters of the field, but at a fearful loss, of which that of Herkimer was not the least. Had the original plan been followed, much of the slaughter would have been spared.

There is no portrait of Herkimer in existence; all that we learn of his appearance was that he was short, stout, and full-faced. He was a man of ability, and, had he survived, from his character and courage he would doubtless have figured creditably in the partisan warfare waged in Eastern and Northern New York, if not in a wider sphere of action.

GENERAL HERKIMER'S RESIDENCE.

THE FIGHT AT ORISKANY.

On the fifth of August, in the morn,
I was ploughing between the rows of corn,
When I heard Dirck Bergen blow his horn.

I let the reins in quiet drop;
I bade my horse in the furrow stop,
And the sweet green leaves unheeded crop.

Down at the fence I waited till
Dirck galloped down the sloping hill,
Blowing his conch-horn with a will.

"Ho, neighbor! stop!" to Dirck I cried,
"And tell me why so fast you ride—
What is the news you scatter wide?"

He drew the rein, and told me then
How, with his seventeen hundred men,
St. Leger vexed the land again.

A fiendish crew around him stood—
The Tory base, the Hessian rude,
The painted prowler of the wood—

The savage Brant was in his train,
Before whose hatchet, quick to brain,
Fell patriot blood in scarlet rain—

THE SITE OF OLD FORT SCHUYLER.

How all this force, to serve the crown,
And win in civil strife renown,
Before Fort Schuyler settled down,

Where Gansevoort close with Willett lay—
Their force too weak for open fray—
Bristling like hunted bucks at bay.

And Dirck, by Herkimer the stout,
Was sent to noise the news about,
And summon all to arm and out.

Far must he spread the word that day,
So, bidding me come to join the fray,
And blowing his horn, he rode away.

I had been married then a year;
My wife to me was doubly dear,
For a child had come our home to cheer.

I had not mingled in the strife
That swept the land; my aim in life
To tend my farm and cheer my wife.

I watched my flocks and herds increase,
And ploughed my land and held my peace:
Men called me the Tory Abner Reece.

Yet now the country needed all
Her manly sons to break her thrall;
Could I be deaf to her piteous call?

I thought me of the cruel foe,
The red-skinned Mingo, skulking low,
The midnight raid, the secret blow—

Hessians and Brunswickers, the lees
Of Europe's cup of miseries,
And brutal Tories, worse than these—

Britons, with rude, relentless hand:
All these made up the cruel band
Which came to spoil and vex the land.

I felt my heart in anger leap—
"No!" cried my spirit from its deep,
"I will not here ignobly creep.

"I have a strong arm for the fray;
I have a rifle sure to slay;
I fear no man by night nor day.

6

"When prowling wolves have left their den,
The hunter's craft is needed then—
The country must not lack for men."

So from the corn-rows green and tall,
I led my plough-horse to the stall,
Then took my rifle from the wall.

I slung my pouch and powder-horn,
I kissed my babe scarce three months born,
And bade my wife farewell that morn.

I journeyed steadily all that day—
Through brake and brier I made my way;
For stream or hill I did not stay.

At set of sun I made my camp
Mid alder bushes thick and damp,
And at the dawn resumed my tramp.

I reached the meeting-place at eight,
But, though no laggard, came too late—
They had not thought for me to wait.

Oh, fatal haste, so soon to stir!
Yet not the fault of Herkimer,
Who knew his foe too well to err.

Rash, headstrong men the others led,
Who mocked at what the general said,
And heaped contumely on his head.

"You know not what you seek," he cried;
"Those are but fools who foes deride;
And prudence dwells with courage tried.

"My messenger left at set of sun;
When once his errand has been done,
Will sound Fort Schuyler's signal-gun.

"Wait till that cannon's voice you hear,
And then we'll fall upon their rear,
As Gansevoort to their van draws near."

Said Colonel Paris, then, "Not so!
We left our homes to strike a blow;
So lead us quickly to the foe.

"Else all may see those do not err
Who brand you as a coward cur
And skulking Tory, Herkimer."

But Herkimer only smiled at first—
He knew those merely words at worst
That from hot-headed rashness burst.

"I have been placed your path to guide,
And shall I lead you, then," he cried,
"To the jaws of ruin gaping wide?"

But Cox replied, "This talk is vain;
If Herkimer fears he may be slain,
Let him in safety here remain."

Flashed Herkimer's eyes with fire at this,
And sank his voice to an angry hiss—
"Such shafts," he cried, "my honor miss.

"March on! but if I judge aright,
You'll find, when comes our foe in sight,
The loudest boaster first in flight."

And so they were marching through a glen
Not far from the mouth of Oriskany, when
I overtook their hindmost men.

I saw Dirck Bergen's honest face
Among the rest; he had reached the place
An hour before me in the race.

He wrung my hand and told me all—
"Look out," said he, "for a rain of ball
And the thickest shower that well can fall.

"For Brant is watching round about,
And long ere this, by many a scout,
He knows his foes are armed and out.

"We'll have it heavily, by-and-by;
But that's no matter—one can but die,
And safer it is to fight than fly."

I laughed a little my fear to hide;
But I felt my memory backward glide
To the home I left on the river-side.

I saw that cabin of logs once more,
The ceiling low and the sanded floor,
And my wife the cradle leaning o'er.

I saw her bending with girlish grace,
And I knew the mother was trying to trace
The father's look in the infant's face.

The house-dog pricked his watchful ear—
He heard some traveller passing near—
She listened my coming step to hear.

But soon dispersed that pleasant scene,
And I glanced with vision clear and keen
Through the close-set boughs of the forest green.

A deep ravine was in our way,
Marshy and damp, and o'er it lay
A causeway formed of logs and clay.

The spot was pleasant—stilly down
Fell forest shadows, cool and brown,
From branch and bough and lofty crown.

Fringing the foreground of the scene,
I saw the slender birches lean
Lovingly o'er the tussocks green.

The leaves were thickly set o'erhead,
The low-growth dense around was spread—
But suddenly filled my heart with dread.

A sight, a sound the soul to shock—
A dark face peering past a rock,
The clicking of a rifle lock.

Forth from a jet of fiery red
Leaped to its mark the deadly lead—
Dirck Bergen fell beside me dead.

To life the sleeping echoes woke,
As from each rock and tree there broke
A flash of fire, a wreath of smoke.

Then rang around us yell on yell,
As though the very fiends of hell
Had risen in that gloomy dell.

And though the foe we scarce could see,
Still from each bush and rock and tree
He poured his fire incessantly.

From a sheltering trunk I glanced around—
Dying and dead bestrewed the ground,
Though some by flight scant safety found.

Ay, flight! as Herkimer had said,
Appalled at blood-drops raining red,
The rear-guard all like dastards fled.

But Herkimer blenched not—clearer, then,
His accents rang throughout the glen,
Cheering the spirits of his men.

And though his horse was slain, and he
Was wounded sorely in the knee,
A cooler man there could not be.

He was not chafed nor stirred the least,
But, gay as a guest at a wedding-feast,
He bade them strip his dying beast.

A famous seat the saddle made
Beneath a beech-tree's spreading shade,
From whence the battle he surveyed.

All through the hottest of the fight
He sat there with his pipe alight,
And gave his orders left and right.

GENERAL HERKIMER DIRECTING THE BATTLE.

Whoever could gaze at him and flee,
The basest of poltroons would be—
The sight chased every fear from me.

None shrank the foe, though sore bestead ;
Each from his tree the bullet sped,
And paid them back with lead for lead.

The battle-shout, the dying groan,
The hatchet's crash, the rifle's tone,
Mixed with the wounded's painful moan.

Full many a stout heart bounding light,
Full many a dark eye beaming bright,
Were still'd in death and closed in night.

I was not idle through the fray ;
But there was one alone that day
I had a fierce desire to slay.

I had seen the face, and marked it well,
That peered from the rock when Bergen fell ;
And I watched for that at every yell.

No hound on scent more rapt could be,
As I scanned the fight from behind the tree ;
And five I slew, but neither was he.

At length I saw a warrior brain
A neighbor's son, young Andrew Lane,
And stoop to scalp the fallen slain.

'Twas he ! my brain to throb began,
My eager hands to the gunstock ran,
And I dropped fresh priming in the pan.

His savage work was speedily through ;
He raised and gave the scalp-halloo ;
Sure aim I took, and the trigger drew.

Off to its mark the bullet sped ;
Leaped from his breast a current red ;
And the slayer of honest Dirck was dead.

Upon us closer now they came ;
We formed in circles walled with flame,
Which way they moved our front the same.

Sore galled and thinned came Butler's men,
With a bayonet charge to clear the glen,
And gallantly we met them then.

Our wrath upon the curs to deal,
There, hand to hand and steel to steel,
We made their close-set column reel.

Fiercely we fought 'mid fire and smoke,
With rifle shot and hatchet stroke,
When over our heads the thunder broke.

And I have heard the oldest say
That ne'er before that bloody day
Such storm was known as stopped our fray.

'Twas one of the cloud-king's victories—
Down came the rain in gusty seas,
Driving us under the heaviest trees.

But short the respite that we got;
The rain and thunder lasted not,
And strife again grew fierce and hot.

At the foot of a bank I took my stand,
To pick out a man from a coming band,
When I felt on my throat a foeman's hand.

At the tightening grasp my eyes grew dim;
But I saw 'twas a Mingo, stout of limb,
And fierce was the struggle I made with him.

Deep peril hung upon my life;
My foot gave way in the fearful strife,
The wretch was o'er me with his knife.

In my hair his eager fingers played,
I felt the keen edge of his blade;
But I struggled the harder undismayed.

I had sunk before his deadly blow,
When suddenly o'er me fell my foe—
A friendly ball had laid him low.

The Mohawks wavered—Brant in vain
Would bring them to the charge again,
For the chiefest of their braves were slain.

We heard a firing far away
In the distance where Fort Schuyler lay—
'Twas Willett with Johnson making play.

MARINUS WILLETT.

Advancing, then, with friendly cries,
A band of patriots met our eyes—
The Tories of Johnson in disguise.

They came as though to aid our band,
With cheerful front and friendly hand—
An artful trick and ably planned.

We hailed their coming with a cheer,
But the keen eye of Gardinier
Saw through their mask as they drew near.

"They think," he cried, "by tricks like these,
To lock our sense and bear the keys—
Look! those are Johnson's Refugees!"

A deadly purpose in us rose;
There might be quarter for our foes
Of Mingo breed, but none for those.

For cabins fired, and old men slain,
And outraged women pleading vain,
Cried vengeance on those sons of Cain.

A hurtling volley made to tell,
And then, with one wild, savage yell,
Resistless on their ranks we fell.

The Mohawks see their allies die;
Dismayed, they raise the warning cry
Of "Oonah!" then they break and fly.

A panic seized the startled foe;
They show no front, they strike no blow,
As through the forest in rout they go.

We could not follow—weak and worn
We stood upon the field that morn;
Never was triumph so forlorn.

For of 'our band who fought that day
One half or dead or wounded lay,
When closed that fierce and fearful fray.

And on that field, ere daylight's close,
We buried our dead, but mourned not those
We laid to rest beside our foes.

Revenge, not grief, our souls possest—
We heaped the earth upon each breast,
And left our brothers to their rest.

WHEN Burgoyne was making the descent from Canada which ended in his capture, he began to fall short of provisions. Having learned that the colonists had a store of cattle, he despatched Lieutenant-colonel Baum, with a force of Hessians, loyalists, and savages, to capture the stock and drive it into camp. There were other ostensible objects, such as feeling the opinion of the country and recruiting the corps of loyalists; but the main object was the capture of the cattle.

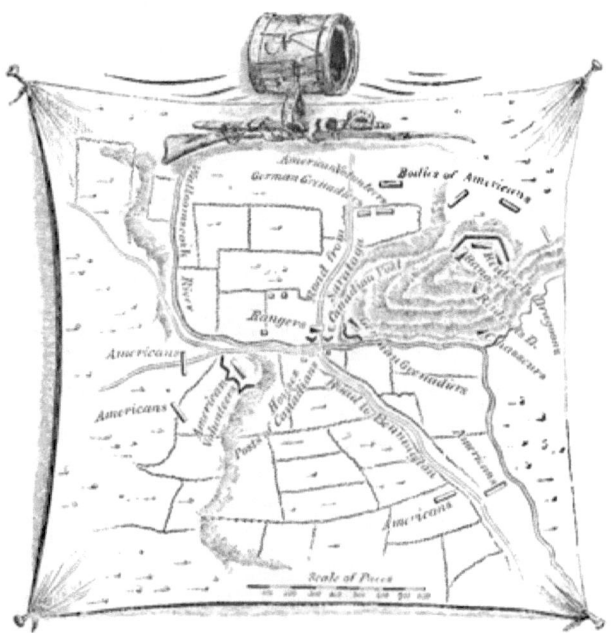

Baum received a sort of roving commission. He was ordered "to scour the country from Rockingham to Otter Creek," to go down the Connecticut to Brattleborough, return by the Albany road, and rejoin Burgoyne, and to impress people with the belief that his force was the advance guard of Burgoyne's army on its way to Boston. He was to arrest all officers or men of the enemy who were found to live off the country, and to impress all the horses in the way, "with as many saddles and bridles as can be found." There were to be thirteen hundred horses, at least, taken, tied in tens for convenience. In short, Baum was to plunder.

The command marched, and on the next day, the 14th of August, 1777, they arrived at the mill on Walloomscoick, after a little skirmish with some Americans who were guarding cattle at Cambridge. Here Baum began to find that his march would not be a holiday parade.

People were uncertain as to the real destination of Burgoyne. He had partially succeeded in convincing many that he meant to march on Boston. The Green Mountain men sent word to

VAN SCHAIK'S MILL.

Exeter imploring aid. The Provincial Assembly of New Hampshire was called hastily together, and its speaker, John Langdon, offered a subsidy of several thousand dollars in hard money to raise and equip troops, and suggested that John Stark should take command. Langdon's words aroused his hearers. Two brigades were raised, one under Whipple and the other under Stark. The latter was then at home. He had distinguished himself at Trenton and Princeton, and had been sent home to direct recruiting. While there, Congress promoted several junior officers, and left his name off. He resigned, but kept up active efforts in behalf of the cause. He accepted the command offered, with the stipulation that he should act at his own discretion; and a part of the brigade raised for him, and a part of Whipple's, was at once placed under his separate command. Men flocked to his support, and at Manchester, twenty miles north of Bennington, he was joined by Colonel Warner, with the remnant of the Vermont men from the disastrous field of Hubbardton. At the same time General Lincoln, who had been ordered to

conduct these new forces to the Hudson River, made his appearance. But Stark refused to yield the command, notwithstanding Congress had passed a resolution that the agreement made between him and New Hampshire was "highly prejudicial to the common cause." He held his position. Hearing of the skirmish at Cambridge, he sent a detachment to meet them. Learning of Baum's advance, he collected all the additional forces possible, and on the morning of the 14th he set forward to support the advance detachment. He soon met the retreating advance under Gregg, and found the enemy posted upon high ground near the Walloomscoick, where they were throwing up hasty intrenchments. Stark fell back to wait for support and plan his action; and Baum, alarmed at the number of the Americans, sent an express to Burgoyne asking for reinforcements. It resulted in Brayman being sent with five hundred men; but they came too late to be of use.

The next day there was a heavy rain, and both sides merely made ready for the fight. The main part of Baum's forces were posted on the high ground, and intrenched as we have stated; but a strong party, principally of Rangers, guarded the ford where the Bennington road crossed. The loyalists, under Peters, had a breastwork on the south side of the river, and a few chasseurs at the mouth of a small water-course. Stark's main body was encamped on the Bennington road.

There had been skirmishing on the 15th, but the rain prevented any active movement. The next morning was clear and

JOHN STARK.

bright, and Stark at once proceeded with his plan. It involved a simultaneous attack of various parties on the intrenchments of the enemy, while the main body under Stark drove the Tories upon the fortified Hessians, and the latter out of their fortified hold. The battle lasted two hours, and in spite of the obstinate bravery of Reidesel's dragoons, led by Baum in person, was won by the Americans. But as soon as this was done, the undisciplined troops began to disperse in search of plunder. Brayman came up with his fresh men, rallied Baum's flying troops, and renewed battle, with every prospect of retrieving the fortunes of the day ; but Colonel Warner's small force coming up and meeting the enemy, with the assistance of the scattered forces Stark was enabled to bring into action, the tide changed again. At sunset the victory was complete. The loss of the Americans was less than two hundred killed and wounded ; of the British, in killed, wounded, and prisoners, nine hundred and thirty-five. Among the spoils were four brass cannon, several hundred stands of arms, two hundred and fifty dragoon swords, and four ammunition wagons.

THE BATTLE OF BENNINGTON.

I see that August morning now before me as I tell
The story of the stirring scenes which I remember well—
The battle-day of Bennington, and what thereon befell.
Yes! we were in the stubble where the hands had gone at dawn,
When, riding swiftly down the road, his dappled gray upon,
Whose flanks were marked with blood and foam, I saw my brother John.
His face was bright, his eyes alight, his bearing proud and high—
" Ho! whither do you speed so fast? Why do you hurry by,
While friends are eager for the news, John Manchester?" said I.

"To fight!" he cried ; "who stays at home upon this August day,
Now Stark has come to Bennington, to lead us in the fray,
Where we may smite these Hessian wolves who babes and women slay?
Let baser men remain at toil, as such have done before,
Let women spin and children play before the farm-house door ;
But till these knaves are driven hence I till the ground no more.
Come you and join me in the strife that Lexington began ;
And as the foe comes down on us, and dares us man to man,
Let you and I acquit ourselves as stout Vermonters can."

The words he uttered on our hearts fell fast in fiery rain ;
The blood in wilder current coursed through artery and vein ;
An impulse there to do and dare went swiftly through each brain.
Our sight and hearing keener grew before his voice's tone—
We saw the cottage roof aflame, the corn-crib overthrown ;
We heard the widow's woful wail, the famished orphan's moan.
We thrilled from heart to finger-tip ; the very air grew red ;
And casting by the tools of toil, off to the house we sped,
To wipe the chambers of our guns and mould the deadly lead.

My mother met me at the door—" James, stay at home!" said she ;
" If you, my youngest born, should fall, what would become of me?
And then, a boy in such a fight of little use can be—"

With that she raised her hand to brush away an oozing tear,
And added—"It was but in June you reached your sixteenth year;
So, while your brother is away, remain to guard us here.
These Hessians whom the king has sent, a hireling war to wage
On children as on bearded men, are ruthless in their rage;
Then go not hence to fall in fight, child of your mother's age."

"Fear not for me," I answered her; "the Hessians I defy;
In years a boy, I know, but then a man in heart am I;
My country needs me in the fight—I cannot more than die.
I come of Abner Manchester, who never knew a fear;
And though as much as any one I hold my mother dear,
I may not on this day of days remain a laggard here.
To herd with women while the fight for freedom is unwon,
While he has sight to mark a foe and strength to bear a gun,
Suits not a stout Green Mountain Boy, nor yet my father's son."

"If you will leave me here alone, so be it!" she replied;
"But take yon firelock from the hooks—it was your father's pride—
He bore it well against the French, nine years before he died—"
As thus she spoke my mother's voice grew tremulous in tone—
"And when you use it, lest your foe in lingering anguish moan,
Sight at a point two fingers' length beneath the collar-bone.
Now, go! my heart, as thus we part, thrills with a mother's pain;
To save you from a single pang, its latest drop I'd drain;
But—show the courage of your sire, or come not here again!"

We started, six of us in all; we made to camp our way,
And found the forces drawn in line, at two o'clock that day,
In front of where, on Walloomscoick, intrenched the foemen lay.
Bold Stark rode slowly down the ranks, with proud, uncovered head—
So quiet we that on the turf we heard his horse's tread—
And at the centre drew his rein, and these the words he said—
"Boys! yonder are the red-coat troops, and, mark me every one,
We win this fight for truth and right, before the day be done,
Or Molly Stark's a widow at the setting of the sun!"

Loud rang the cheering in reply, but through the ranks there ran
A murmur, for they felt it long until the fight began,
Although they knew the tardiness was from a well-formed plan.

For in their hurried council there our leaders planned the fight,
That Herrick with three hundred men should march upon their right,
And Nichols on the left with more spared from our scanty might,
To join their forces in the rear, and there assault begin,
While we upon their front advanced at signal of the din ;
And then let those who dealt their blows with fiercest vigor win.

Our forces stood without a stir, in silence grim and dark,
While like a statue on his steed so motionless sat Stark,
When suddenly, with finger raised, the general whispered—" Hark !"
We stood as silent as the grave, and as we bent to hear,
Above the silence far away there came a lusty cheer ;
Some shots were fired—we knew our friends had joined upon their rear—
" Now, hearts so warm, move like the storm !" said Stark, and led the way ;
"Green Mountain Boys, acquit yourselves like mettled men to-day !
Take careful aim and waste no lead ! the wolves are brought to bay !"

Then came the crash of musketry loud pealing on my ear ;
I heard a whizzing sound go past—down fell a comrade near—
There was a throbbing in my breast that seemed almost like fear—
A shock, to see a stout young man, in all his youth and pride,
One who had left the day before a fond and blooming bride,
Thus done to death, the scarlet blood slow trickling from his side ;
And doubly strange that fearful sight to one who ne'er before,
Amid the shouting of the hosts, and the cannon's deadly roar,
Had seen a fellow-mortal lie thus lifeless in his gore.

But rage supplanted this at once—my heart grew strong again ;
Uprose grim wrath and bitter hate, and bitterer disdain.
I longed to add a leaden drop unto that whizzing rain—
The tenderness of youth I found forevermore had gone.
My cheek was leaned upon my gun, the sight was finely drawn
Upon a gold-laced officer who cheered the Hessians on ;
And, trembling in my eagerness to strike for home a blow,
I sent the lead, as mother said, two fingers' length below
The ridge that marked the collar-bone, and laughed when fell the foe.

There comes a pause within the fight—we see some horsemen group,
And on the breastwork ridge take line, a dark and threatening troop—
Compact they form, with sabres drawn, upon our force to swoop.

Oh, now we smile a grimly smile, and wrath our bosom stirs;
We newly load and careful prime our firelocks for the curs—
For well we know their uniform, those Brunswicker chasseurs!
They come at last whose doom was past long, weary months before—
They come to meet the death that we to deal upon them swore
When first the bearded robbers came for plunder to our shore.

They come, the mercenary dogs, assassins of the crown;
Right gracefully and gallantly they sit their horses brown,
Then rowel-deep they drive their spurs, and thunder madly down.
But as the ground is shaking round before their horses' tread,
A sheet of fire their sabres lights, high waving overhead,
And of the hundred men who charge full forty-eight lie dead.
Those who survive in vain they strive; they may not fight nor run—
We pass them quickly to the rear, our captives every one.
And so we serve the Brunswicker that day at Bennington.

Then where their remnant lay at bay our angry torrent rolled—
As when a dam gives way, and leaves the waters uncontrolled—
Sweeping to break the square of steel in centre of their hold.
No peal of trump nor tap of drum our eager footsteps timed;
With firelocks clubbed or knife in hand, our faces powder-grimed,
Fatigue unfelt and fear unknown, the ridge of earth we climbed;
Down from its crest we fearless plunged amid the smoke clouds dun,
But struck no blow upon the foe—resistance there was none—
Down fell their arms, uprose the white, and Bennington was won.

Then greeted we surviving friends, and mourned for those who fell,
And, leaning on our firelocks, heard the tales that soldiers tell
How comrades whom they little knew had done their duty well,
And how amid the hosts in fight no coward had been found;
Then gazed upon the foemen slain that lay in heaps around,
And said, in bitter hate and scorn, they well became the ground—
So evermore by sea and shore might those invaders be,
Who came with chains for limbs of men who by their birth were free—
A pang shot sharply through my brain—my brother! where was he?

I sought and found him with the blood slow oozing from his brain;
His feet were pointed to the ridge, his back was to the plain,
And round him in a curving row a dozen Hessians slain.

How well his sword had mown was shown in gazing at the heap—
Strown like a swathe of grass before some lusty mower's sweep—
Of those whose souls had fled their forms through bloody wounds and deep.
I placed his corse upon his horse, and gently homeward led
The wearied steed that ne'er before was ridden by the dead ;
And we buried the corse in the meadow with a white stone at its head.

THE BATTLE-GROUND OF BENNINGTON.

7

LIEUTENANT-GENERAL BURGOYNE.

[From an English Print, 1783.]

THE way for the operations which resulted in the capture of Burgoyne and his forces was mainly prepared by General Schuyler, who was unjustly replaced by Gates. The battles at Stillwater rendered the result a certainty. The surrender of Burgoyne and his forces, by showing the probability of success, secured the French alliance. The value of that consisted in the fact that it gave Great Britain more to do, and prevented her from crushing the new States, which had declared their independence from "the State of Great Britain." Up to that time Louis the Sixteenth had only given us covert assistance. Then he, unwisely for himself, declared war against England, leading to a train of events which crystallized the memory of long years of oppression of the French people into revolution. The king did not foresee the consequences. Joseph the Second of Austria was more shrewd. When urged to join the alliance against Great Britain he said—"I am a sovereign, and will not aid to injure my own trade." The material assistance afforded by France was slight, and at Savannah injurious. The French were at Yorktown, but Cornwallis would have fallen without their aid. Afterwards they not only claimed the laurels, but affected to consider us as a French dependency, and carried it so far as to provoke us to war. We owe France nothing; but we owe much to the memory of the Marquis de la Fayette, who generously placed at our disposal his life and fortune; who was our disinterested friend at a critical period and throughout; and who will be remembered with gratitude so long as the Union remains.

Whether Arnold distinguished himself at the first battle of Stillwater may be a moot question. That he was a moving spirit in the second battle is undoubted. The victory was very much due to his exertions. Up to the time of his treason, despite his rapacity and extravagance at Philadelphia, he merited praise for his dash, bravery, and unflinching devotion to the cause of Independence. That he was treated badly by the Congress is true; but that is scarcely a palliation of his infamous conduct in revenge. The Congress seems to have had a faculty for injustice. As it acted towards Arnold, so it did to Paul Jones, John Stark, and Philip Schuyler. But none of the last named revenged themselves by treason. The contrast between the conduct of Arnold and Schuyler is particularly notable. The latter had managed affairs with dexter-

HORATIO GATES.

ity, and it was to his prudence, decision, and skill that the surrender of Burgoyne was mainly due. At the last moment he was superseded by Gates, under circumstances calculated to arouse his resentment. Schuyler, unlike Arnold, was not merely a patriot, but a man of honor. He was ready to submit to wrong rather than betray the cause. The conduct of Arnold was the baser from the fact that Washington, who felt that the man had been wronged, labored to do him right, and had placed him in the responsible command of West Point, to pave the way to that distinction his services on the battle-field deserved. Arnold, therefore, added ingratitude and breach of confidence to treason. He seems to have had the courage of a bull-dog, but to have been totally lacking in moral principle.

When I was a boy I met an old Revolutionary soldier who had served under Arnold. He would praise him for his bravery in one minute, and denounce his treachery the next, rarely speaking of him without tears. Hence the idea of the ballad.

BENEDICT ARNOLD.

ARNOLD AT STILLWATER.

Ah! you mistake me, comrades, to think that my heart is steel,
Cased in a cold endurance, nor pleasure nor pain to feel;
Cold as I am in my manner, yet over these cheeks so seared
Tear-drops have fallen in torrents, thrice since my chin grew beard.

Thrice since my chin was bearded I suffered the tears to fall:
Benedict Arnold, the traitor! he was the cause of them all.
Once, when he carried Stillwater, proud of his valor I cried;
Then, with my rage at his treason—with pity when André died.

Benedict Arnold, the traitor, sank deep in the pit of shame,
Bartered for vengeance his honor, blackened for profit his fame;
Yet never a gallanter soldier, whatever his after-crime,
Fought on the red field of honor than he in his early time.

Ah! I remember Stillwater as it were yesterday:
Then first I shouldered a firelock, and set out the foemen to slay.
The country was up all around us, racing and chasing Burgoyne,
And I had gone out with my neighbors, Gates and his forces to join.

Marched we with Poor and with Learned, ready and eager to fight;
There stood the foemen before us, cannon and men on the height.
Onward we trod with no shouting, forbidden to fire till the word;
As silent their long line of scarlet—not one of them whispered or stirred

"FIVE TIMES WE CAPTURED THEIR CANNON, AND FIVE TIMES THEY TOOK THEM AGAIN."

Suddenly, then, from among them smoke rose and spread on the breeze;
Grape-shot flew over us sharply, cutting the limbs from the trees;
But onward we pressed till the order of Cilley fell full on the ear,
Then we levelled our pieces and fired them, and rushed up the slope with
     a cheer.

Fiercely we charged on their centre, and beat back the stout grenadiers,
And wounded the brave Major Ackland, and grappled the swart cannoneers.
Five times we captured their cannon, and five times they took them again;
But the sixth time we had them we kept them, and with them a share of
     their men.

Our colonel who led us dismounted, high on a cannon he sprang;
Over the noise of our shouting clearly his joyous words rang:
"These are our own brazen beauties! Here to America's cause
I dedicate each, and to freedom!—foes to King George and his laws!"

Worn as we were with the struggle, wounded and bleeding and sore,
Some stood all pale and exhausted, some lay there stiff in their gore;
And round through the mass went a murmur that grew to a whispering clear,
And then to reproaches outspoken—"If General Arnold were here!"

For Gates, in his folly and envy, had given the chief no command,
And far in the rear some had seen him horseless and moodily stand,
Knitting his forehead in anger, and gnawing his red lip in pain,
Fretting himself like a blood-hound held back from his prey by a chain.

Hark! at our right there is cheering! there is the ruffle of drums!
Here is the well-known brown charger! Spurring it madly he comes!
Learned's brigade have espied him, rending the air with a cheer:
Woe to the terrified foeman, now that our leader is here!

Piercing the tumult behind him, Armstrong is out on his track:
Gates has despatched his lieutenant to summon the fugitive back.
Armstrong might summon the tempest, order the whirlwind to stay,
Issue commands to the earthquake—would they the mandate obey?

Wounds, they were healed in a moment, weariness instantly gone:
Forward he pointed his sabre—led us, not ordered us on.
Down on the Hessians we thundered, he, like a madman, ahead:
Vainly they strove to withstand us; raging, they shivered and fled.

On to their earthworks we drove them, shaking with ire and dismay;
There they made stand with a purpose to beat back the tide of the day.
Onward we followed, then faltered; deadly their balls whistled free.
Where was our death-daring leader? Arnold, our hope, where was he?

He? He was everywhere riding! hither and thither his form,
On the brown charger careering, showed us the path of the storm;
Over the roar of the cannon, over the musketry's crash,
Sounded his voice, while his sabre lit up the way with its flash.

Throwing quick glances around him, reining a moment his steed—
"Brooks! that redoubt!" was his order: "let the rest follow my lead!

Mark where the smoke-cloud is parting! see where their gun-barrels glance!
Livingston, forward! On, Wesson! charge them! Let Morgan advance!"

"Forward!" he shouted, and, spurring on through the sally-port then,
Fell sword in hand on the Hessians, closely behind him our men.
Back shrank the foemen in terror, off went their forces pell-mell,
Firing one Parthian volley: struck by it, Arnold he fell.

"FIRING ONE PARTHIAN VOLLEY."

Ours was the day. Up we raised him; spurted the blood from his knee—
"Take this cravat, boys, and bind it; I am not dead yet," said he.
"What! did you follow me, Armstrong? Pray, do you think it quite right,
Leaving your duties out yonder to risk your dear self in the fight?"

"General Gates sent his orders—" faltering the aide-de-camp spoke—
"You're to return, lest some rashness—" Fiercely the speech Arnold broke:
"Rashness! Why, yes! tell the general the rashness he dreaded is done!
Tell him his kinsfolk are beaten! tell him the battle is won!"

Oh, that a soldier so glorious, ever victorious in fight,
Passed from a daylight of honor into the terrible night;
Fell as the mighty archangel, ere the earth glowed in space, fell—
Fell from the patriot's heaven down to the loyalist's hell!

In 1771, a stockade fort was erected at the mouth of Wheeling Creek, in what was then the district of West Augusta, in Virginia, to protect the settlers against a threatened invasion of the savages. It was called Fort Fincastle, and is said to have been planned by George Rogers Clarke. The original garrison was twenty-five men; but though this was afterwards ordered to be doubled, it is doubtful if the command were ever obeyed. In 1776, when the colonists rebelled against the crown, and West Augusta was divided into the counties of Ohio, Youghiogheny, and Monongahela, the name was changed to Fort Henry, in honor of Patrick Henry, then governor of Virginia.

The organization of Ohio County at this time was essentially military, every able-bodied man being enrolled; and this enrollment was a list of taxables, and formed the basis of the county revenue. David Shepherd, the colonel commanding the county militia, was also the presiding justice of the county court. Besides this the county had to raise two companies as a part of the Continental Army. These were commanded respectively by Captains John Lemmon and Silas Zane; but as they appear never to have enlisted more than twenty men, the project was probably abandoned.

Fort Henry was the only fortified place capable of a protracted defence, though there were block-houses in the settlements at Peach

GEORGE ROGERS CLARKE.

Bottom, Grave Creek, Short Creek, and Cross Creek. It stood on high ground a short distance above the mouth of Wheeling Creek, and near it were twenty or thirty log-houses, the beginning of what is now the flourishing city of Wheeling. The famous attack upon it was made in September, 1777. During the spring of that year frequent aggressions had been made upon the white settlements by thieving bands of Indians, and these attacks had been either repulsed or the marauders followed up and chastised. During the summer these increased, and the result was a cessation of ordinary occupations, and an understood placing of the country under martial law. At the beginning of September it was learned that Simon Girty, a notorious white renegade, was raising a strong band of Wyandots, Mingoes, and Shawanock—mainly of the former. So well did their leader manage, however, that he brought his band, from four to five hundred in number, to the walls of Fort Henry before his real points of attack were known.

On the night of the 26th of September, a small scouting party discovered smoke arising at the south of Wheeling Creek. Captain Ogle, one of these, thought it came from the burning of the block-house at Grave Creek; and Colonel Shepherd sent out to ascertain the truth, and caused the families living around to take refuge in the fort. The next morning his scouts sent to warn neighboring settlements were fired on, and one of them killed, by six lurking Indians. A party of fifteen, sent to dislodge these, encountered the main force, and all but three were killed. A party sent to their aid, lost two-thirds of their number. These losses cut down the garrison to twelve men and boys. The assailing force, which now closely invested the garrison, was never estimated at less than three hundred and eighty, but was probably much more.

During the whole of the day the fight was maintained with great vigor. The Indians at one time made an impromptu cannon of a huge log, winding it around with chains from the black-smith's shop in the village, loading it with round stones, and directing it against the gate of the fort. It exploded, and killed and wounded several of the besiegers. The next morning, relief came in the shape of forty men, under M'Culloch, from Short Creek, and fourteen more from Cross Creek. The enemy burned the houses around, carried off the cattle, and, bearing their dead, moved away.

During the fight, the defenders grew short of powder. There was a keg in Ebenezer Zane's house about sixty yards away, and this was obtained by the sister of Ebenezer, a young woman, in the way described in the ballad.

BETTY ZANE.

Women are timid, cower and shrink
At show of danger, some folk think;
But men there are who for their lives
Dare not so far asperse. their wives.
We let that pass—so much is clear,
Though little dangers they may fear,
When greater perils men environ,
Then women show a front of iron;
And, gentle in their manner, they
Do bold things in a quiet way,
And so our wondering praise obtain,
As on a time did Betty Zane.

A century since, out in the West,
A block-house was by Girty pressed—
Girty, the renegade, the dread
Of all that border, fiercely led
Five hundred Wyandots, to gain
Plunder and scalp-locks from the slain;
And in this hold—Fort Henry then,
But Wheeling now—twelve boys and men
Guarded with watchful ward and care
Women and prattling children there,
Against their rude and savage foes,
And Betty Zane was one of those.

There had been forty-two at first
When Girty on the border burst;

But most of those who meant to stay
And keep the Wyandots at bay,
Outside by savage wiles were lured,
And ball and tomahawk endured,
Till few were left the place to hold,
And some were boys and some were old ;
But all could use the rifle well,
And vainly from the Indians fell,
On puncheon roof and timber wall,
The fitful shower of leaden ball.

Now Betty's brothers and her sire
Were with her in this ring of fire,
And she was ready, in her way,
To aid their labor day by day,
In all a quiet maiden might.
To mould the bullets for the fight,
And, quick to note and so report,
Watch every act outside the fort ;
Or, peering from the loop-holes, see
Each phase of savage strategy—
These were her tasks, and thus the maid
The toil-worn garrison could aid.

Still, drearily the fight went on
Until a week had nearly gone,
When it was told—a whisper first,
And then in loud alarm it burst—
Their powder scarce was growing ; they
Knew where a keg unopened lay
Outside the fort at Zane's—what now?
Their leader stood with anxious brow.
It must be had at any cost,
Or toil and fort and lives were lost.
Some one must do that work of fear ;
What man of men would volunteer?

Two offered, and so earnest they,
Neither his purpose would give way ;
And Shepherd, who commanded, dare
Not pick or choose between the pair.

But ere they settled on the one
By whom the errand should be done,
Young Betty interposed, and said,
"Let me essay the task instead.
Small matter 't were if Betty Zane,
A useless woman, should be slain ;
But death, if dealt on one of those,
Gives too much vantage to our foes."

Her father, smiled with pleasure grim—
Her pluck gave painful pride to him ;
And while her brothers clamored "No !"
He uttered, " Boys, let Betty go !
She'll do it at less risk than you ;
But keep her steady in your view,
And be your rifles shields for her.
If yonder foe make step or stir,
Pick off each wretch who draws a bead,
And so you'll serve her in her need.
Now I recover from surprise,
I think our Betty's purpose wise."

The gate was opened, on she sped ;
The foe astonished, gazed, 'tis said,
And wondered at her purpose, till
She gained that log-hut by the hill.
But when, in apron wrapped, the cask
She backward bore, to close her task,
The foemen saw her aim at last,
And poured their fire upon her fast.
Bullet on bullet near her fell,
While rang the Indians' angry yell ;
But safely through that whirring rain,
Powder in arms, came Betty Zane.

They filled their horns, both boys and men,
And so began the fight again.
Girty, who there so long had stayed,
By this new feat of feet dismayed,
Fired houses round and cattle slew,
And moved away—the fray was through.

But when the story round was told
How they maintained the leaguered hold,
It was agreed, though fame was due
To all who in that fight were true,
The highest meed of praise, 'twas plain,
Fell to the share of Betty Zane.

A hundred years have passed since then ;
The savage never came again.
Girty is dust ; alike are dead
Those who assailed and those bestead.
Upon those half-cleared, rolling lands,
A crowded city proudly stands ;
But of the many who reside
By green Ohio's rushing tide,
Not one has lineage prouder than
(Be he or poor or rich) the man
Who boasts that in his spotless strain
Mingles the blood of Betty Zane.

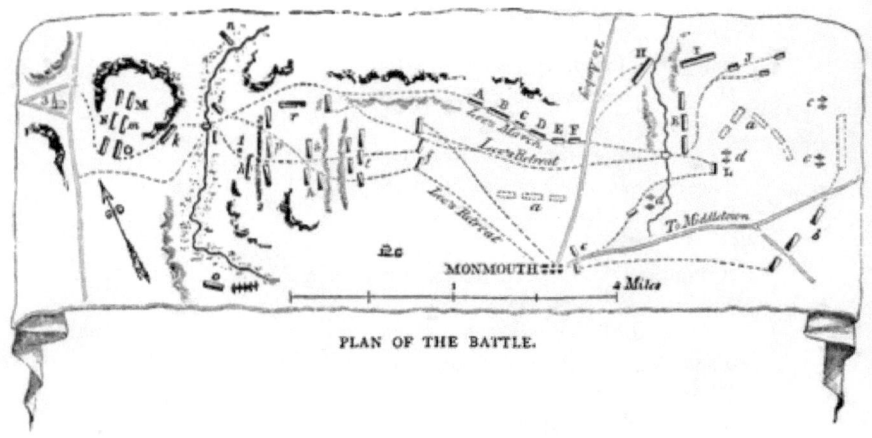

PLAN OF THE BATTLE.

OPERATIONS AT MONMOUTH.

IN June, 1777, the American army was still encamped at Valley Forge. Instructions had been sent from England to Sir Henry Clinton, who replaced Howe as commander-in-chief, to evacuate Philadelphia, and make New York the centre of his operations. So prudently did he prepare for this step that Washington knew nothing of his intention until the British army was actually over the Delaware. A council of war held at Valley Forge decided adversely to an attack upon the enemy, but Washington took up the pursuit, determined to act according to circumstances. He sent Arnold, who was incapacitated for action in the field, with a small detachment to take possession of Philadelphia, while he crossed the river at Coryell's Ferry, above Trenton. Clinton, who had to build bridges all along his route, and who was encumbered with baggage and stores, so that on the single effective road he found his train was twelve miles long, was slow in his movements. This, somehow, produced an impression that he meant to draw on a general engagement. An American council of war was called at Hopewell, which still opposed a battle, but recommended harassing the enemy by detachments. Washington ordered Morgan's corps to the British right flank, Maxwell's brigade to the left, and Scott's picked corps, with some forces under Dickinson and Cadwallader, to annoy them on flanks and rear.

Clinton's first plan was to strike New Brunswick and embark at the Raritan; but at Allentown, finding Washington in his way, and disinclined to a general engagement under the circumstances, he moved to the right, intending to pass Monmouth Court-house and embark at Sandy Hook. The Americans were now at Kingston. Lee and all the general officers, except La Fayette, Greene, and Wayne, were in favor of continuing the system of annoyance; but Washington at last made ready for a battle. He ordered forward Wayne with a thousand men to support the troops most in advance, giving La Fayette the command of the advanced force—about four thousand in all—while he moved the main body towards Cranberry. On the morning of the 27th, La Fayette arrived at Englishtown. By this time Clinton had made a different disposition of his forces, throwing his grenadiers to his rear, and placing the encumbrances in front under charge of Knyphausen. He made his camp in a strong position near the court-house, in a line three miles in length, protected by woods and marshes. This forced Washington to support his advance strongly, and he sent Lee forward to join La Fayette with two brigades at Englishtown, which placed Lee in command then as senior officer. The corps of Morgan still threatened the enemy's right, and Dickinson's force his left. Washington, fearing the enemy would take post on Middletown Heights, determined to attack the rear on a movement in that direction, and sent orders to Lee to prepare for an assault.

The next day, the 28th, was Sunday, and bade fair to be, as it became, one of the hottest days of the season. An hour after midnight, Lee ordered Dickinson forward with a strong party of ob-

servation, and directed Morgan to attack the British as soon as they moved. The rest of the troops were ordered to prepare to march, and before dawn, Scott and Varnum's brigades were moving slowly towards the court-house; at day-break, Knyphausen, with his Hessians and loyalists; and at eight o'clock Clinton followed with the main body. The whole American army was put in motion, and Lee received orders to attack, unless he saw very powerful reasons otherwise. This discretionary clause had like to have resulted in defeat. Dickinson having received word that the British were about to attack with the main force, which was incorrect, sent the news to Lee, who believed it. He pushed forward across the morass to a narrow road near the parsonage, and joined Dickinson on the heights. Here the news brought was conflicting, and while Lee was trying to get it correctly, Lafayette came up with the rest of the advanced corps. Learning that the enemy was not in force on either flank, he marched on. He had between five and six thousand men, including those under Morgan and Dickinson. He pressed forward, under cover of the woods, formed a part of his line for action, and rode

LAFAYETTE IN 1777.

forward with Wayne far enough to see that the British deploying on the left were merely a heavy covering party. Hoping to cut them off from the main army, he detached Wayne with seven hundred men and two field-pieces to make a feint in the rear.

About nine o'clock, the Queen's Dragoons being observed on a height, apparently preparing to attack, Lee ordered the light-horse to let them nearly approach, and then to fall back on Wayne. This manœuvre would have succeeded, had not a small party under Butler fired at them from ambush, which caused them to fall back. Wayne ordered the artillery to open on them, and then charged, Oswald opening fire from an eminence in the morass. Wayne was attacking with vigor, when to his chagrin he received an order from Lee to move less vigorously, lest he might prevent the latter from cutting off the covering party. Wayne obeyed, but Lee brought his forces from under cover in detachments only. Sir Henry Clinton, fearing that the Americans were massing on both flanks for the purpose of capturing his baggage, faced about to attack Lee, and force those threatening his flanks to come to the latter's aid. Lafayette seeing this, asked permission of Lee to attempt gaining the

GENERAL WAYNE.

rear of the enemy. Lee refused at first, but finally agreed to let him attack the enemy's left; but weakened Lafayette by withdrawing three regiments to the support of the right. Riding

HENRY KNOX.

forward to reconnoitre, Lee saw, or thought he saw, a heavy force marching on the Middletown road towards the court-house. He ordered the right to fall back. The British were advancing with the apparent design of gaining the American rear, just as Scott and Maxwell's brigades were approaching the enemy's right, the former forming for action. Lee ordered both to fall back, arrange their line in the woods, and await orders. Mistaking the nature of the order, they retreated through the woods towards Freehold meeting-house. As soon as Lee learned this, instead of recalling them, he sent word to Lafayette to fall back on the court-house, which he obeyed, the enemy pursuing him as far as the latter place, where they halted. Both parties suffered from the extreme heat, their men in some instances dropping exhausted. Lee made one stand, and then resumed his retreat. It degenerated into a panic. Numbers were lost in the morass—few perished by ball. There was little firing on either side.

During this time Washington was moving to Lee's support. For Lee, when he discovered the large covering party in the enemy's rear, and had planned to cut them off, sent word to the commander-in-chief of his purpose. On the receipt of this message, Washington had despatched Greene with the right wing by Freehold Meeting-house, to prevent the enemy turning that flank, while he prepared to move the left in the rear of Lee, in support. Suddenly came the news that Lee was retreating, with Clinton in pursuit. Washington was astounded. There had been little firing to indicate battle, and, riding forward, he met the head of the retreating force. Halting it, he pushed on and found Lee at the head of the second column. He demanded in an angry way the meaning of the confusion, and Lee, who also lost his temper, replied harshly. A few hasty and bitter words passed, when Washington rode on, stayed the troops, and ordered Oswald to check the progress of the enemy with his cannon. The men under Stewart and Ramsay were formed in battle order. Then

Washington turned to the chafed Lee, and said, "Will you command in that place, sir?" Lee replied in the affirmative. "Then," said Washington, "I expect you to attack the enemy immediately." "Your command shall be obeyed, sir," replied Lee, "and I will not be the first to leave the field."

While Washington was bringing order out of the confusion elsewhere, and disposing properly of Greene's forces, and the left wing under Stirling, Lee vigorously carried out his orders; but the force of the enemy was too overwhelming. After a vigorous fight, he brought them under cover of a fire by Ogden, detailed for that purpose, he being "the last to leave the field," and forming

FREEHOLD MEETING-HOUSE.

them in line on the slope, reported to Washington for further orders. Washington seeing the men were worn out, ordered him to arrange them at Englishtown, while he attacked with the main body. The action now became hot all along the line, and was pursued with varying success, until at length, towards sunset, the British army, badly worsted, fell back upon the heights held by Lee in the morning. It was a strong position, flanked by forest and morass, but Wash-

BATTLE-GROUND AT MONMOUTH.

ington prepared to attack it. The darkness coming on, the men were ordered to sleep on their arms, and to move at daylight.

But this was unneeded. At midnight, Clinton silently stole off; and when dawn came he was so far away towards New Brunswick, that pursuit was useless. The Americans lost in the battle sixty-seven killed, one hundred and sixty wounded, and one hundred and thirty missing; but a number of the last had been merely prostrated by the extreme heat, and afterward rejoined their commands. There were two hundred and forty-nine of the British left dead on the field, of whom fifty-nine died of sunstroke. The number of their wounded is unknown.

BATTLE OF MONMOUTH.

Four-and-eighty years are o'er me; great-grandchildren sit before me;
  These my locks are white and scanty, and my limbs are weak and worn;
Yet I've been where cannon roaring, firelocks rattling, blood outpouring,
  Stirred the souls of patriot soldiers, on the tide of battle borne;
Where they told me I was bolder far than many a comrade older,
    Though a stripling at that fight for the right.

All that sultry day in summer beat his sullen march the drummer,
  Where the Briton strode the dusty road until the sun went down;
Then on Monmouth plain encamping, tired and footsore with the tramping,
  Lay all wearily and drearily the forces of the crown,
With their resting horses neighing, and their evening bugles playing,
    And their sentries pacing slow to and fro.

Ere the day to night had shifted, camp was broken, knapsacks lifted,
  And in motion was the vanguard of our swift-retreating foes;
Grim Knyphausen rode before his brutal Hessians, bloody Tories—
  They were fit companions, truly, hirelings these and traitors those—
While the careless jest and laughter of the teamsters coming after
    Rang around each creaking wain of the train.

'Twas a quiet Sabbath morning; nature gave no sign of warning
  Of the struggle that would follow when we met the Briton's might;
Of the horsemen fiercely spurring, of the bullets shrilly whirring,
  Of the bayonets brightly gleaming through the smoke that wrapped the fight;
Of the cannon thunder-pealing, and the wounded wretches reeling,
    And the corses gory red of the dead.

Quiet nature had no prescience; but the Tories and the Hessians
  Heard the baying of the beagles that were hanging on their track;
Heard the cries of eager ravens soaring high above the cravens;
  And they hurried, worn and worried, casting startled glances back,
Leaving Clinton there to meet us, with his bull-dogs fierce to greet us,
    With the veterans of the crown, scarred and brown.

For the fight our souls were eager, and each Continental leaguer,
  As he gripped his firelock firmly, scarce could wait the word to fire;
For his country rose such fervor, in his heart of hearts, to serve her,
  That it gladdened him and maddened him and kindled raging ire.
Never panther from his fastness, through the forest's gloomy vastness,
    Coursed more grimly night and day for his prey.

I was in the main force posted; Lee, of whom his minions boasted,
  Was commander of the vanguard, and with him were Scott and Wayne.
What they did I knew not, cared not; in their march of shame I shared not;
  But it startled me to see them panic-stricken back again,
At the black morass's border, all in headlong, fierce disorder,
    With the Briton plying steel at their heel.

Outward cool when combat waging, howsoever inward raging,
  Ne'er had Washington showed feeling when his forces fled the foe;
But to-day his forehead lowered, and we shrank his wrath untoward,
  As on Lee his bitter speech was hurled in hissing tones and low:
"Sir, what means this wild confusion? Is it cowardice or collusion?
    Is it treachery or fear brings you here?"

WASHINGTON REBUKING LEE.

Lee grew crimson in his anger—rang his curses o'er the clangor,
  O'er the roaring din of battle, as he wrathfully replied;
But his raging was unheeded; fastly on our chieftain speeded,
  Rallied quick the fleeing forces, stayed the dark, retreating tide;
Then, on foaming steed returning, said to Lee, with wrath still burning,
  "Will you now strike a blow at the foe?"

At the words Lee drew up proudly, curled his lip and answered loudly :
  "Ay !" his voice rang out, "and will not be the first to leave the field ;"
And his word redeeming fairly, with a skill surpassed but rarely,
  Struck the Briton with such ardor that the scarlet column reeled ;
Then, again, but in good order, past the black morass's border,
    Brought his forces rent and torn, spent and worn.

As we turned on flanks and centre, in the path of death to enter,
  One of Knox's brass six-pounders lost its Irish cannoneer ;
And his wife who, 'mid the slaughter, had been bearing pails of water
  For the gun and for the gunner, o'er his body shed no tear.
"Move the piece !"—but there they found her loading, firing that six-pounder,
    And she gayly, till we won, worked the gun.

Loud we cheered as Captain Molly waved the rammer ; then a volley
  Pouring in upon the grenadiers, we sternly drove them back ;
Though like tigers fierce they fought us, to such zeal had Molly brought us
  That, though struck with heat, and thirsting, yet of drink we felt no lack :
There she stood amid the clamor, busily handling sponge and rammer,
    While we swept with wrath condign on their line.

From our centre backward driven, with his forces rent and riven,
  Soon the foe re-formed in order, dressed again his shattered ranks ;
In a column firm advancing, from his bayonets hot rays glancing
  Showed in waving lines of brilliance as he fell upon our flanks,
Charging bravely for his master : thus he met renewed disaster
    From the stronghold that we held back repelled.

Monckton, gallant, cool, and fearless, 'mid his bravest comrades peerless,
  Brought his grenadiers to action but to fall amid the slain ;
Everywhere their ruin found them ; red destruction rained around them
  From the mouth of Oswald's cannon, from the musketry of Wayne ;
While our sturdy Continentals, in their dusty regimentals,
    Drove their plumed and scarlet force, man and horse.

Beamed the sunlight fierce and torrid o'er the battle raging horrid,
  Till, in faint exhaustion sinking, death was looked on as a boon ;
Heat, and not a drop of water—heat, that won the race of slaughter,
  Fewer far with bullets dying than beneath the sun of June ;
Only ceased the terrible firing, with the Briton slow retiring,
    As the sunbeams in the west sank to rest.

MOLLY PITCHER.

On our arms so heavily sleeping, careless watch our sentries keeping,
  Ready to renew the contest when the dawning day should show;
Worn with toil and heat, in slumber soon were wrapt our greatest number,
  Seeking strength to rise again and fall upon the wearied foe;
For we felt his power was broken: but what rage was ours outspoken
    When, on waking at the dawn, he had gone.

In the midnight still and sombre, while our force was wrapt in slumber,
  Clinton set his train in motion, sweeping fast to Sandy Hook;
Safely from our blows he bore his mingled Britons, Hessians, Tories—
  Bore away his wounded soldiers, but his useless dead forsook;
Fleeing from a worse undoing, and too far for our pursuing:
    So we found the field our own, and alone.

How that stirring day comes o'er me! How those scenes arise before me!
  How I feel a youthful vigor for a moment fill my frame!
Those who fought beside me seeing, from the dim past brought to being,
  By their hands I fain would clasp them—ah! each lives but in his name;
But the freedom that they fought for, and the country grand they wrought for,
    Is their monument to-day, and for aye.

THERE is scarcely a native of Bergen County, in New Jersey, who has not heard of Jack, the Regular, and by the older residents there are still told a number of stories of his cruelty and rapacity. That there was such a person, that he was an active loyalist during the Revolutionary war, and that he was finally killed by the Van Valens, and his lifeless body brought into Hackensack in a wagon, there seems to be no doubt. But with all my industrious endeavor I have never been able to get particulars as to his family, the date of his birth, or when he was killed. I find that his real name was John Berry, and that he managed to gain rank as a captain—probably of loyalists. His nickname arose from a boast he made that he was no marauder, but held a regular commission from his Gracious Majesty. Hence those who sided with the Americans called him Jack, the Regular, and he was scarcely ever known by another name.

So far as I can learn he was killed on the slope of the Palisade ridge, not far from what is known as the Ridgefield station, on the Northern Railroad, and by a long shot. It was merely fired in vexation by Van Valen, who was astonished when the partisan fell, and hesitated for some time to verify the fact of his death. Jack's band at that time had been broken up, or he was in some disgrace; for he had had apparently no command for some time before he was killed, and was with but one companion at the time.

JACK, THE REGULAR.

In the Bergen winter night, when the hickory fire is roaring,
Flickering streams of ruddy light on the folk before it pouring;
When the apples pass around, and the cider passes after,
And the well-worn jest is crowned by the hearers' hearty laughter,
When the cat is purring there, and the dog beside her dozing,
And within his easy-chair sits the grandsire old, reposing,
Then they tell the story true to the children hushed and eager,
How the two Van Valens slew, on a time, the Tory leaguer,
             Jack, the Regular.

Near a hundred years ago, when the maddest of the Georges
Sent his troops to scatter woe on our hills and in our gorges,
Less we hated, less we feared, those he sent here to invade us
Than the neighbors with us reared who opposed us or betrayed us;
And amid those loyal knaves who rejoiced in our disasters,
As became the willing slaves of the worst of royal masters,

Stood John Berry, and he said that a regular commission
Set him at his comrades' head ; so we called him, in derision,
     "Jack, the Regular."

When he heard it—"Let them fling ! Let the traitors make them merry
With the fact my gracious king deigns to make me Captain Berry.
I will scourge them for the sneer, for the venom that they carry ;
I will shake their hearts with fear, as the land around I harry ;
They shall find the midnight raid waking them from fitful slumbers ;
They shall find the ball and blade daily thinning out their numbers ;
Barn in ashes, cattle slain, hearth on which there glows no ember,
Neatless plough and horseless wain—thus the rebels shall remember
     Jack, the Regular.

Well he kept his promise then, with a fierce, relentless daring,
Fire to roof-trees, death to men, through the Bergen valleys bearing.
In the midnight deep and dark came his vengeance darker, deeper—
At the watch-dog's sudden bark woke in terror every sleeper ;
Till at length the farmers brown, wasting time no more on tillage,
Swore these ruffians of the crown, fiends of murder, fire, and pillage,
Should be chased by every path to the dens where they had banded,
And no prayers should soften wrath when they caught the bloody-handed
     Jack, the Regular.

One by one they slew his men : still the chief their chase evaded ;
He had vanished from their ken, by the fiend or fortune aided—
Either fled to Paulus Hoek, where the Briton yet commanded,
Or his stamping-ground forsook, waiting till the hunt disbanded.
So they stopped pursuit at length, and returned to toil securely—
It was useless wasting strength on a purpose baffled surely ;
But the two Van Valens swore, in a patriotic rapture,
They would never give it o'er till they'd either kill or capture
     Jack, the Regular.

Long they hunted through the wood, long they slept upon the hill-
    side ;
In the forest sought their food, drank when thirsty at the rill-side ;
No exposure counted hard—theirs was hunting border fashion ;
They grew bearded like the pard, and their chase became a passion.
Even friends esteemed them mad, said their minds were out of balance,
Mourned the cruel fate, and sad, fallen on the poor Van Valens.

But they answered to it all, "Only wait our loud view-holloa
When the prey shall to us fall; for to death we mean to follow
          Jack, the Regular.

Hunted they from Tenavlie to the shore where Hudson presses
On the base of trap-rocks high; through Moonachie's damp recesses;
Down as far as Bergen Hill; by the Ramapo and Drochy,
Overproek and Pellum Kill—meadows flat and hill-top rocky—
Till at last the brothers stood where the road from New Barbadoes
At the English Neighborhood slants towards the Palisadoes;
Still to find the prey they sought leave no sign for hunter eager;
Followed steady, not yet caught was the skulking, fox-like leaguer,
          Jack, the Regular.

Who are they that yonder creep by those bleak rocks in the distance,
Like the figures born in sleep, called by slumber to existence?
Tories, doubtless, from below—from the Hoek sent out for spying.
"No! the foremost is our foe—he so long before us flying!
Now he spies us! See him start! wave his kerchief like a banner,
Lay his left hand on his heart in a proud, insulting manner.
Well he knows that distant spot past our ball—his low scorn flinging—
If you can not feel the shot, you shall hear the firelock's ringing,
          Jack, the Regular."

Ah! he falls! An ambuscade? 'Twas impossible to strike him.
Are there Tories in the glade? Such a trick is very like him.
See! his comrade by him kneels, turning him in terror over,
Then takes nimbly to his heels. Have they really slain the rover?
It is worth some risk to know; so, with firelocks poised and ready,
Up the sloping hill they go, with a quick lookout, and steady.
Dead! The random shot had struck, to the heart had pierced the
   Tory—
Vengeance seconded by luck! Lies there cold and stiff and gory
          Jack, the Regular.

"Jack, the Regular, is dead! Honor to the man who slew him!"
So the Bergen farmers said as they crowded round to view him.
For the wretch that lay there slain had, with wickedness unbending,
To their roofs brought fiery rain, to their kinsfolk woful ending.
Not a mother but had prest, in a sudden pang of fearing,
Sobbing darlings to her breast when his name had smote her hearing;

Not a wife that did not feel terror when the words were uttered ;
Not a man but chilled to steel when the hated sounds he muttered—
      "Jack, the Regular."

Bloody in his work was he, in his purpose iron-hearted ;
Gentle pity could not be when the pitiless had parted ;
So the corse in wagon thrown with no decent cover o'er it—
Jeers its funeral rites alone—into Hackensack they bore it,
'Mid the clanging of the bells in the old Dutch church's steeple,
And the hooting and the yells of the gladdened, maddened people.
Some they rode and some they ran by the wagon where it rumbled,
Scoffing at the lifeless man, all elate that Death had humbled
      Jack, the Regular.

Thus within the winter night, when the hickory fire is roaring,
Flickering streams of ruddy light on the folk before it pouring ;
When the apples pass around, and the cider follows after,
And the well-worn jest is crowned by the hearers' hearty laughter ;
When the cat is purring there, and the dog beside her dozing,
And within his easy-chair sits the grandsire old, reposing,
Then they tell the story true to the children hushed and eager,
How the bold Van Valen slew, on a time, the Tory leaguer,
      Jack, the Regular.

AFTER his disaster at Camden, Gates was superseded in the command of the Southern Departments by Greene, to whom he turned over the remnant of his army, about two thousand men

BANASTRE TARLETON.

in all. Of these a force of a thousand, or less, were placed in Union District, near the junction of the Broad and Pacolet rivers, nearly fifty miles to the left of Greene's position. Lord Cornwallis at once determined to attack and destroy this detachment, and sent Tarleton, with eleven hundred men, including his own cavalry and two field-pieces, for that purpose. Morgan's forces, outside of Howard's Continentals and Washington's dragoons, were raw militia, some of whom had never seen battle, had had little drill, and were devoid of discipline. The task was supposed to be easy, and Tarleton began his march in high spirits. In consequence of bad roads he was much delayed on the march, and it was not until the 15th of January, 1781, four days after starting, that he drew near the Pacolet. Morgan, finding his forces not sufficient to stop the enemy at the river, retreated and took post on the north side of Thickety Mountain, near the Cowpens. Tarleton at once pushed on in pursuit, leaving his baggage behind, riding all night, and at eight o'clock of the morning of the 17th came in sight of the American patrol. Fearing they might escape he ordered an immediate attack. To his surprise he found Morgan prepared to give battle.

It is unnecessary to expand this note further, since the movements in the battle are given with accuracy in the ballad. The pursuit of the British was not relinquished until they reached the open wood near or about the point where the fight first began. The remnant of Tarleton's force, by the next morning, reached Cornwallis's camp. The American loss was twelve killed and about forty-eight wounded. Cornwallis's report to Sir Henry Clinton gives the British loss at one hundred killed and five hundred and twenty-three prisoners. The Americans captured the two field-pieces, two standards, eight hundred muskets, thirty-five baggage-wagons, and one hundred dragoon horses. The battle was not so important itself but in its consequences. It contributed very much towards the capture of Cornwallis.

DANIEL MORGAN.

THE BATTLE OF THE COWPENS.

To the Cowpens riding proudly, boasting loudly, rebels scorning,
    Tarleton hurried, hot and eager for the fight;
From the Cowpens, sore confounded, on that January morning,
    Tarleton hurried somewhat faster, fain to save himself by flight.

In the morn he scorned us rarely, but he fairly found his error
    When his force was made our ready blows to feel;
When his horsemen and his footmen fled in wild and pallid terror
    At the leaping of our bullets and the sweeping of our steel.

All the day before we fled them, and we led them to pursue us,
    Then at night on Thickety Mountain made our camp;
There we lay upon our rifles, slumber quickly coming to us,
    Spite the crackling of our camp-fires and our sentries' heavy tramp.

Morning on the mountain border, ranged in order, found our forces,
    Ere our scouts announced the coming of the foe;
While the hoar-frost lying near us, and the distant watercourses,
    Gleamed like silver in the sunlight, seemed like silver in their glow.

Morgan ranged us there to meet them, and to greet them with such favor
    That they scarce would care to follow us again;
In the rear the Continentals—none were readier nor braver;
    In the van, with ready rifles, steady, stern, our mountain men.

Washington, our trooper peerless, gay and fearless, with his forces
    Waiting panther-like upon the foe to fall,
Formed upon the slope behind us, where, on rawboned country horses,
    Sat the sudden-summoned levies brought from Georgia by M'Call.

Soon we heard a distant drumming, nearer coming, slow advancing—
    It was then upon the very nick of nine;
Soon upon the road from Spartanburg we saw their bayonets glancing,
    And the morning sunlight playing on their swaying scarlet line.

In the distance seen so dimly they looked grimly; coming nearer
    There was naught about them fearful, after all,

Until some one near me spoke, in voice than falling water clearer,
  "Tarleton's quarter is the sword-blade, Tarleton's mercy is the ball."

Then the memory came unto me, heavy, gloomy, of my brother
  Who was slain while asking quarter at their hand;
Of that morning when was driven forth my sister and my mother,
  From our cabin in the valley by the spoilers of the land.

I remembered of my brother slain, my mother spurned and beaten,
  Of my sister in her beauty brought to shame;
Of the wretches' jeers and laughter, as from mud-sill up to rafter
  Of the stripped and plundered cabin leaped the fierce, consuming flame.

WILLIAM WASHINGTON.

But that memory had no power there in that hour there to depress me—
  No! it stirred within my spirit fiercer ire;
And I gripped my sword-hilt firmer, and my arm and heart grew stronger;
  And I longed to meet the wronger on the sea of steel and fire.

On they came, our might disdaining, where the raining bullets leaden
  Pattered fast from scattered rifles on each wing;
Here and there went down a foeman, and the ground began to redden;
  And they drew them back a moment, like the tiger ere his spring.

Then said Morgan, "Ball and powder kill much prouder men than George's;
  On your rifles and a careful aim rely.
They were trained in many battles—we in workshops, fields, and forges;
  But we have our homes to fight for, and we do not fear to die."

Though our leader's words we cheered not, yet we feared not; we awaited,
  Strong of heart, the threatened onset, and it came:
Up the sloping hill-side swiftly rushed the foe so fiercely hated;
  On they came with gleaming bayonet 'mid the cannon-smoke and flame.

At their head rode Tarleton proudly; ringing loudly o'er the yelling
  Of his men we heard his voice's brazen tone;
With his dark eyes flashing fiercely, and his sombre features telling
  In their look the pride that filled him as the champion of the throne.

On they pressed, when sudden flashing, ringing, crashing, came the firing
  Of our forward line upon their close-set ranks;
Then at coming of their steel, which moved with steadiness untiring,
  Fled our mountaineers, re-forming in good order on our flanks.

Then the combat's ranging anger, din, and clangor, round and o'er us
  Filled the forest, stirred the air, and shook the ground;
Charged with thunder-tramp the horsemen, while their sabres shone be-
    fore us,
  Gleaming lightly, streaming brightly, through the smoky cloud around.

Through the pines and oaks resounding, madly bounding from the mountain,
  Leaped the rattle of the battle and the roar;
Fierce the hand-to-hand engaging, and the human freshet raging
  Of the surging current urging past a dark and bloody shore.

Soon the course of fight was altered; soon they faltered at the leaden
  Storm that smote them, and we saw their centre swerve.
Tarleton's eye flashed fierce in anger; Tarleton's face began to redden;
  Tarleton gave the closing order—"Bring to action the reserve!"

Up the slope his legion thundered, full three hundred; fiercely spurring,
  Cheering lustily, they fell upon our flanks;
And their worn and wearied comrades, at the sound so spirit-stirring,
  Felt a thrill of hope and courage pass along their shattered ranks.

By the wind the smoke-cloud lifted lightly, drifted.to the nor'ward,
　　And displayed in all their pride the scarlet foe;
We beheld them, with a steady tramp, and fearless, moving forward,
　　With their banners proudly waving, and their bayonets levelled low.

Morgan gave his order clearly—"Fall back nearly to the border
　　Of the hill, and let the enemy come nigher!"
Oh! they thought we had retreated, and they charged in fierce disorder,
　　When out rang the voice of Howard—"To the right about, face!—Fire!"

JOHN. E. HOWARD.

Then upon our very wheeling came the pealing of our volley,
　　And our balls made red a pathway down the hill;
Broke the foe, and shrank and cowered; rang again the voice of Howard—
　　"Give the hireling dogs the bayonet!"—and we did it with a will.

In the mean while one red-coated troop, unnoted, riding faster
　　Than their comrades, on our rear in fury bore;
But the light-horse led by Washington soon brought it to disaster,
　　For they shattered it and scattered it, and smote it fast and sore.

Like a herd of startled cattle from the battle-field we drove them;
　　In disorder down the Mill-gap road they fled;
Tarleton led them in the racing, fast he fled before our chasing,
　　And he stopped not for the dying and he stayed not for the dead.

Down the Mill-gap road they scurried and they hurried with such fleetness—
  We had never seen such running in our lives!
Ran they swifter than if seeking homes to taste domestic sweetness,
  Having many years been parted from their children and their wives.

Ah! for some no wife to meet them, child to greet them, friend to shield
  them!
  To their home o'er ocean never sailing back;
After them the red avengers, bitter hate for death had sealed them,
  Yelped the dark and red-eyed sluthhound unrelenting on their track.

In their midst I saw one trooper, and around his waist I noted
  Tied a simple silken scarf of blue and white;
When my vision grasped it clearly to my hatred I devoted
  Him, from all the hireling wretches who were mingled there in flight.

For that token in the summer had been from our cabin taken
  By the robber-hands of wrongers of my kin;
'Twas my sister's—for the moment things around me were forsaken;
  I was blind to fleeing foemen, I was deaf to battle's din.

Olden comrades round me lying dead or dying were unheeded;
  Vain to me they looked for succor in their need;
O'er the corses of the soldiers, through the gory pools I speeded,
  Driving rowel-deep my spurs within my madly bounding steed.

As I came he turned, and staring at my glaring eyes he shivered;
  Pallid fear went quickly o'er his features grim;
As he grasped his sword in terror, every nerve within him quivered,
  For his guilty spirit told him why I solely sought for him.

Though the stroke I dealt he parried, onward carried, down I bore him—
  Horse and rider—down together went the twain:
"Quarter!"—He! that scarf had doomed him! stood a son and brother
  o'er him;
  Down through plume and brass and leather went my sabre to the brain—
  Ha! no music like that crashing through the skull-bone to the brain.

THE massacre at Cherry Valley, New York, was notably cruel and bloody. In November, 1778, Walter Butler, with two hundred loyalists, and Joseph Brant, with five hundred Indians, swept down on the place, and commenced an indiscriminate slaughter. The very loyalists among the inhabitants were not spared. John Wells was well affected to the crown, yet he and

JOSEPH BRANT.

his family, with the exception of his son John, who happened to be in Schenectady, were killed. Jane Wells was very much esteemed for her kindness and other good qualities. The elder Wells was a particular friend of Colonel John Butler, Walter's father, who said, when he heard of his death, "I would have gone miles on my hands and knees to have saved that family, and why my son did not do it God only knows." One loyalist, Peter Smith, who had formerly been a servant in the family, tried to save Miss Jenny, but the Indian who had seized her struck her on the head with his tomahawk and killed her. One man by the name of Mitchell was at a distance, saw the savages approaching, and finding that he could not rejoin his family, escaped into the woods. On his return he found his house burning, and near it lay the bodies of his wife and four children. One of these, a little girl, was still living, when he saw a party approach. He dropped the child, and secreted himself behind a tree. One of the new-comers saw the child to be alive yet, and stooping, brained her with a hatchet. The wretch was not an Indian, but a white loyalist savage named Newbery, who was afterwards hanged as a spy by General James Clinton. Brant saved a number of prisoners, and would have spared the women and children, but Walter Butler denied all appeals for mercy.

Butler's time was to come. On the 22d of August, 1781, Colonel Willet attacked a force of five hundred loyalists and Indians at Johnstown, and defeated them. They were commanded by Major Ross and Walter Butler. The remnant of the enemy retreated all that night, and could not be overtaken. It was during that retreat that Butler was killed in the manner related in the ballad. Skenando, the Oneida chief, who is supposed to have been his slayer, was about seventy-four years old at the time. He lived many years after, dying at the age of one hundred and ten, on March 19, 1816. His burial was attended by a large number of citizens. A short time before his death he said to a visitor, who made some inquiries about his age, "I am an old hemlock. The winds of a hundred winters have whistled through my top. The generation to which I belonged has gone and left me. Pray to my Jesus that I may have patience to wait for my appointed time to die."

DISTANT VIEW OF CHERRY VALLEY.

DEATH OF WALTER BUTLER.

I.

Overhead the sky of morning
    Gives of goodly weather sign;
From the milking to the meadows
    Slowly go the lowing kine.

Fall in sparks of fire the dew-drops
    From the overburdened leaves;
Flit from bough to bough the peewees;
    Hum the mud-wasps at the eaves.

Mists that recent wrapped the valley
    Now are sweeping o'er the hills;
And the broad red sun is casting
    Gold upon the lakes and rills.

Deep and brown and sombre shadows
　　Creep the forest trees between;
Here and there the shades of crimson
　　Speck the liquidambars' green.

Lo! a horseman swiftly rising
　　From between the river's banks;
Dust is on the rider's garments,
　　Blood upon his horse's flanks.

At the portal of the tavern
　　Hard he draws the bridle-rein,
For a moment, feet in stirrup,
　　One refreshing draught to drain.

What can make the village dwellers,
　　In a hushed and breathless group,
Gather round that jaded horseman
　　By the village-tavern stoop?

To him come the anxious mothers,
　　Bearing babes upon their arms;
Close behind them crowd the maidens,
　　Yet unscathed by love's alarms. . .

Near him gather stalwart farmers,
　　Sturdy, strong, and sun-embrowned;
And the curious village children,
　　Play suspending, stand around.

Breathless all, until the horseman,
　　Mug in hand, has told his tale;
Then around there spreads a murmur
　　Like the warning of the gale.

Now it lulls and now it rises,
　　Like the patter of the rain—
"Heaven at last has dealt its vengeance!
　　Walter Butler has been slain!"

II.

Never tongue may tell the horror
  Of that dark November day,
When through startled Cherry Valley
  Walter Butler took his way—

Walter Butler and his Tories,
  With the savage Brant in train,
Marking every rod of progress
  By the bodies of the slain.

Walter Butler! cruel panther,
  Lapping tongue in human gore ;
Even Brant, the bloody Mohawk,
  Had of truth and pity more.

His the will to save the helpless
  From the tomahawk and ball,
Had not you with rage forbade him,
  Saying, "Curse them! kill them all!"

Even boyhood's old companions,
  Comrades of your later days,
Friends who, seeing not your vices,
  Gave your scanty virtues praise—

None of these could gain your mercy
  On that long-remembered day ;
For the stranger, friend or foeman,
  Came one doom relentless—"Slay!"

Swiftly at your word the hatchet
  Crashed into the quivering brain,
And the swarthy fiends in fury
  Tore the scalp-skins from the slain.

Gray-haired elders, whom your father
  Knew as friends in days of yore,
You had joy to see their corses
  Welter in their oozing gore.

9

Mothers lying mangled, dying,
  In their throes made deeper moans
As they saw the skulls of infants
  Shattered on the ruthless stones.

These, and shrieks of fleeing maidens,
  Speechless children's pleading tears,
And the yelling of the savage,
  Made sweet music to your ears.

Bloody Walter Butler! owning
  Brain of fire and heart of stone,
Twenty deaths, could you endure them,
  Would not for these deeds atone.

Nevermore may come your victims
  To the pleasant earth again—
Never hear the blessed tidings—
  "Walter Butler has been slain!"

III.

When the savage had departed,
  Careless of the woe he caused,
Then, amid the smouldering ruins,
  An Oneida came and paused.

He was tall and gaunt and aged,
  Crowned his head with films of snow;
For the frosts of seventy winters
  Thus had honored Skenando.

Gazed he on the work of evil,
  Which around its traces spread,
On the blood which stained the herbage,
  On the pale and mangled dead.

"I have been," so spake the chieftain,
  "Forty years the white man's friend;
So have been to Walter Butler—
  Would have proved so to the end.

"Cruel son of lying father,
  Faithless, too, as this may show,
You shall rue the dreadful doing
  Which creates in me a foe.

"Here are friends—I knew and loved them,
  Proved them often in my need.
Great Monedo's curse be on you,
  Walter Butler, for this deed.

"Here, by all his bitter sorrow,
  By his scant and whitened hairs,
By the spirits of the fallen,
  Thus the old Oneida swears :

"He will follow in your pathway,
  He will hang upon your track,
Through the hurry of the foray,
  Through the battle's awful rack,

"Till at length his keen-edged hatchet,
  Driven to your coward brain,
With its crashing voice shall utter,
  'Walter Butler has been slain!'"

IV.

In the waste of Cherry Valley
  Desolation long was seen,
Seated on the heaps of ashes
  Where the home of man had been.

Desolation there was sitting,
  Brooding on the fearful past,
Crouching in the murky shadows
  Of her sullen pinions vast.

There, amid the thorny briers,
  Mingled with the earth and stones,
Hidden by the noxious herbage,
  Were the weather-whitened bones.

On the branches of the maples
  Sat the houseless cocks, and crowed;
In the forest's dark recesses
  Starveling watch-dogs made abode.

Through the copse-wood, snorting, scampered
  Herds of wild and savage swine;
And with yellow deer there wandered
  What survived among the kine.

In the fenceless fields the panther
  Crouched to spring upon his prey;
And the rattlesnake lay basking
  Careless in the public way.

Where had stood the barn and stable,
  And the garden with its bees;
Where the house, with peakèd gable,
  Peeped through groves of locust-trees;

Where the children, newly risen,
  Peered at sunrise through the pane,
But through which the murdered children
  Nevermore may peer again;

Where the housewife in the morning,
  Pail in hand, the fountain near,
Stopped to gossip with her neighbors,
  And the village news to hear;

Where the farmers in the porches
  Sat at closing of the day,
Smoking pipes whose odors mingled
  With the fragrance of the hay;

Where at eve the cows were lowing
  Answer to the milkmaid's cry;
And, with hens about him, proudly
  Sultan Spurs came strutting by;

Where the horses in the pasture,
  On the fence's topmost rail,
Crossed their necks and loudly whinnied,
  Some tired traveller's horse to hail;

Where the rooting swine at footsteps
  Raised their heads beneath the trees,
And the watch-dog bayed defiance
  To the murmur of the breeze—

Clouds that overhung the valley
  Would not melt in gentle rain;
They were waiting for the tidings—
  "Walter Butler has been slain!"

V.

Where the Canada so swiftly
  Through the mountain gorges flows,
Walter Butler found the mercy
  He had dealt to hapless foes.

He had fought that day with Willet,
  And the battle had been lost,
For our men the past remembered,
  To the ruthless Tories' cost.

No one there would seek for quarter,
  No one mercy would bestow;
From the wrath that swept around them,
  Flight alone could save the foe.

Butler, baffled, fled the combat
  On his charger tried and good,
Through the glen and o'er the valley,
  Through the gap within the wood.

Rode he steadily and swiftly,
  While a swart and angry pack
Of the hound-like, wild Oneidas
  Yelped in anger on his track.

On the Canada was rushing,
   Tempest-swollen, from the hills,
Maddened with the furious urging
   Of a hundred surging rills.

But he heeded not its raging;
   At the danger fear was lost.
In he spurred his panting charger,
   And the foaming river crossed.

On its bank a moment halting,
   To the foes upon his track
Words and motions of defiance
   Butler hurled, exulting, back.

On his hot and spent pursuers
   Thus his words of scorning fell:
"He who rides with Walter Butler
   Sits a steed that carries well.

"In the battle and the foray
   Human blood shall fall like rain,
Ere you carry round the tidings—
   'Walter Butler has been slain!'"

VI.

As he waved his hand in mocking
   Came the whizzing of the ball;
Loudly shouted the Oneidas
   As they saw the braggart fall.

Then the white-haired chief who led them
   Flung his powder-horn aside,
And his rifle dropped, preparing
.   For a leap within the tide.

"Skenando!" exclaimed a comrade,
   "Stay! the stream runs fierce and wild;
And your age will make you weaker
   In its current than a child.

"For the youngest there is danger
  Ere he'd reach the farther shore,
From the raging of the waters,
  And the rocks o'er which they pour."

"Stay me not!" he answered, sternly;
  "Vengeance to the flood impels;
Hear you not the dying moaning
  Of the murdered Jenny Wells?"

Plunging in the yellow torrent
  With his tomahawk in hand,
Swam the chief of the Oneidas,
  Struggling till he reached the land—

Till upon the green bank's summit,
  Close beside the shaded wood,
O'er the sorely wounded Butler
  With a purpose fierce he stood.

Said the pallid, craven butcher,
  "Let my ransom save my head;
I can give you gold if living,
  I am profitless if dead!"

Skenando replied, "With fever
  I in Cherry Valley lay,
Where a white man nursed and healed me,
  Clothed and sent me on my way.

"That same white man had a daughter;
  She with you in childhood played;
Yet one day, when leaves had fallen,
  By your orders died the maid.

"The Oneida, sworn to vengeance,
  Stands prepared to keep his vow;
Think of Jenny Wells and tremble!
  Ah! you ask no mercy now.

"Wretch! remember Cherry Valley!"
  Sank the Tory with a groan,
And the fierce and vengeful savage
  Drove his hatchet through the bone.

.   .   .   .   .

Back returned the swart Oneidas
  Ere the setting of the sun ;
And the scalp of Walter Butler
  Dangled from the belt of one.

To the stout, victorious soldiers
  Who so well that day had fought,
And were now at ease reposing,
  Pleasant was the news they brought.

When was told around the camp-fire
  How the hatchet clave the brain,
Oh, how joyous was the shouting—
  "Walter Butler has been slain."

From the narrative of a survivor of the gallant men who participated in the fight at King's Mountain I wrote the ballad, and aimed to give it the simple style of the narrator. But the old man, perfectly truthful in intent, fell into some errors. He omits all mention of the M'Dowells. Colonel M'Dowell was not in the battle. He objected to fighting a battle without a general officer, and he was despatched in search of one. While gone, the rest elected Colonel Campbell to command, and got to work. Major M'Dowell however remained, and commanded the regiments. He calls Shelby, Evan Shelby. But Evan Shelby, who was Isaac's father, and who distinguished himself at Point Pleasant, was not at King's Mountain.

The official account of the battle transmitted to Gates, and probably the correct one, is as follows :

"On receiving intelligence that Major Ferguson had advanced up as high as Gilbert Town, in Rutherford County, and threatened to cross the mountains to the Western waters, Colonel William Campbell, with four hundred men, of Washington County, of Virginia, Colonel Isaac Shelby, with two hundred and forty men from Sullivan County, of North Carolina, and Lieuten-

ant-colonel Sevier, with two hundred and forty men, of Washington County, of North Carolina, assembled at Watauga, on the twenty-fifth day of September, where they were joined by Colonel Charles M'Dowell, with one hundred and sixty men, from the counties of Burke and Rutherford, who had fled before the enemy to the Western waters. We began our march on the twenty-sixth, and on the thirtieth we were joined by Colonel Cleaveland, on the Catawba River, with three hundred men, from the counties of Wilkes and Surrey. No one officer having properly the right to the command-in-chief, on the first of October we despatched an express to Major-general Gates, informing him of our situation, and requested him to send a general officer to take command of the whole. In the mean time, Colonel Campbell was chosen to act as commandant, till such general officer should arrive. We marched to the *Cowpens*, on Broad River, in South Carolina, where we were joined by Colonel James Williams, with four hundred men, on the evening of the sixth of October, who informed us that

COLONEL ISAAC SHELBY.

the enemy lay encamped somewhere near the Cherokee Ford, off Broad River, about thirty miles distant from us. By a council of principal officers, it was then thought advisable to pursue the enemy that night with nine hundred of the best horsemen, and have the weak horse and foot men to follow us as fast as possible. We began our march with nine hundred of the best men about eight o'clock the same evening, and, marching all night, came up with the enemy about three o'clock P.M. of the seventh, who lay encamped on the top of King's Mountain, twelve miles north of the Cherokee Ford, in the confidence that they could not be forced from so advantageous a post. Previous to the attack on our march, the following disposition was made : Colonel Shelby's regiment formed a column in the centre on the left ; Colonel Campbell's regiment another on the right, with part of Colonel Cleaveland's regiment, headed in front by Major

Joseph Winston; and Colonel Sevier's formed a large column on the right wing. The other part of Cleaveland's regiment, headed by Colonel Cleaveland himself, and Colonel Williams's regiment, composed the left wing. In this order we advanced, and got within a quarter of a mile of the enemy before we were discovered. Colonel Shelby's and Colonel Campbell's regiments began the attack, and kept up a fire on the enemy, while the right and left wings were advancing to surround them, which was done in about five minutes, when the fire became general all around. The engagement lasted an hour and five minutes, the greater part of which a heavy and incessant fire was kept up on both sides. Our men, in some parts where the regulars fought, were obliged to give way a distance, two or three times, but rallied and returned with additional ardor to the attack. The troops upon the right having gained the summit of the eminence, obliged the enemy to retreat along the summit of the ridge to where Colonel Cleaveland commanded, and were there stopped by his brave men. A flag was immediately hoisted by Captain Depeyster, the commanding officer (Major Ferguson having been killed a little before), for a surrender. Our fire immediately ceased, and the enemy laid down their arms (the greater part of them charged) and surrendered themselves prisoners at discretion. It appears from their own provision returns for that day, found in their camp, that their whole force consisted of eleven hundred and twenty-five men, out of which they sustained the following loss:

"Of the regulars, one major, one captain, two sergeants, and fifteen privates killed; thirty-five privates wounded, left on the ground not able to march; two captains, four lieutenants, three ensigns, one surgeon, five sergeants, three corporals, one drummer, and forty-nine privates taken prisoners.

"Loss of the Tories: two colonels, three captains, and two hundred and one killed; one major and one hundred and twenty-seven privates wounded, and left on the ground not able to march. One colonel, twelve captains, eleven lieutenants, two ensigns, one quartermaster, one adjutant, two commissaries, eighteen sergeants, and six hundred privates taken prisoners.

"Total loss of the enemy, eleven hundred and five men at King's Mountain.

"Given under our hands at camp.

"BENJA. CLEAVELAND,
ISAAC SHELBY,
WM. CAMPBELL."

KING'S MOUNTAIN BATTLE-GROUND.

THE BATTLE OF KING'S MOUNTAIN.

I.

You ask your grandsire hoary
  To tell you of the day,
When, in his lusty manhood's prime,
  To fight he took his way.

So here beside our cabin,
  Deep in the Baptist Vale,
While sinks the sun within the west,
  And light begins to fail—

Upon the lofty summit,
  Before the set of sun,
I'll tell you how by mountaineers
  The battle-field was won.

II.

In Southern Carolina
  Cornwallis settled down;
And Forguson twelve hundred led,
  In pride from Gilbert Town.

For Gates was crushed at Camden,
  And only Marion's band
Lay, but a remnant of itself,
  Within the low swamp-land.

The cause was hid in darkness,
  And few expected dawn,
For strength had fled, and fire was dead,
  And even hope was gone.

Then spoke old Evan Shelby
  To Campbell and Sevier—
"Shall base maurauders revel thus,
  As we sit idle here?

"Up steep and stern King's Mountain
 Went Forguson, I learn;
Should men take heart to deal a blow,
 He never would return.

"Out then and scour the counties,
 Our forces shall combine,
And, ready for the battle, cross
 The Carolina line."

Said gallant William Campbell—
 "I'm with you there, old friend;
Though borne by numbers to the earth,
 We will not break nor bend.

"Three hundred western hunters
 I volunteer to bring,
All loyal to their country's cause,
 Though rebel to the king.

"All hardy western hunters,
 Who serve for love, not hire;
Each prompt to mark the foeman dark,
 And drop him when they fire."

Sevier was in their counsel—
 "Three hundred I can bring
To meet these savage myrmidons
 Of George, our former king.

"Each man is firm and fearless,
 Each uses rifle well;
Nor sabre-stroke, nor musket-ball,
 Upon our ranks may tell.

"From home or over ocean
 They fear no haughty foes—"
'Twas thus he boasted of his band,
 And I was one of those.

Then word went out that Shelby,
  With Campbell and Sevier,
Against the common enemy
  Would lead the mountaineer.

With moccasons corked, and rifles
  New flinted every one,
Right soon a thousand brave and strong
  Were gathered at Doe Run.

To them came Cleaveland's forces,
  When once they left the glen,
And mounted on their own good steeds
  Rode sixteen hundred men.

Campbell, as chief commander,
  The centre column led ;
And with him Shelby's regiment,
  With Shelby at its head.

The left was led by Cleaveland,
  The right obeyed Sevier ;
And like the sky which bent o'erhead
  Each brow was calm and clear.

Then this laconic order
  Was passed both left and right—
"*Tie overcoats, pick touch-holes, prime,
  And ready be for fight!*"

We neared where they stood waiting,
  And cleft our force in three ;
And then dismounting, to the limbs
  Tied horses silently.

The centre up the mountain
  Pressed eager to the fight,
While round the base, to gain his rear,
  The wings swept left and right.

In calm and deadly silence,
  With firm and steady tramp,
On pressed our three divisions towards
  The centre of their camp.

Then came their muskets' rattle,
  And comrades at my side,
Whom I had known for many years,
  Were stricken down, and died.

Uriah Byrne, of Black Fork,
  A younger man than I—
His hot blood spurting in my face—
  Fell at my feet to die.

And swarthy Robin Harper,
  Whose house was nigh to mine,
Pierced by a bullet, fell and left
  A wife and orphans nine.

And golden-haired John Bowen,
  A boy scarce past sixteen—
I knew his mother ere his birth,
  And few so fair I've seen—

A woman fair and stately,
  Who loved her husband well,
And mourned, nor ever wedded more,
  When he in battle fell.

She sent with us this stripling,
  And thus to him she said,
"Return with honor to your home,
  Or stay among the dead.

"You are the stay and comfort
  Of my declining years;
That I am loath to part with you,
  Witness these bitter tears.

"But now these foul invaders
  Sweep hill and valley o'er,
Go! drive them from these mountains free,
  Or see my face no more!"

And there I saw his ringlets
  Lie, bloody, on his cheek;
I caught his eye, and stooped to hear
  The words that he might speak.

"A message to my mother,
  If you survive the day:
And say her darling son was still
  The foremost in the fray.

"My spirit to my Maker
  I yield, and trust that He
Forgives my sins for sake of Him
  Who died upon the tree.

"Yet 'tis a thing of terror,
  When youthful hopes are bright,
And youthful blood flows full and free,
  To bid the world good-night.

"Go, comrade, to your duty,
  And leave me here to die—"
His pulses stopped, I turned away,
  I had no time to sigh.

But filled with sudden fury,
  I joined the strife again,
Nor paused to watch the fight around
  Till I three foes had slain—

One for my early schoolmate,
  One for my neighbor old,
And one for him with golden hair
  That lay so stark and cold.

The foe raised shouts exulting;
  We answered not at all;
But still with steady coolness poured
  Our rain of rifle-ball.

But hark! a voice is ringing
  As clearly as a drum—
'Tis Forguson's—"Charge bayonet!
  And drive the rebel scum!"

III.

Down gallantly and boldly
  The British soldiers came,
When on their wall of bristling steel
  We hurled our scorching flame.

They paused a single moment,
  And then they broke and fled;
But Forguson re-formed their ranks,
  Proud riding at their head.

They fell on us like panthers
  In laurel roughs at bay,
And at their front, compact and firm,
  The Cleaveland men gave way.

But ere a rod they drove them,
  Sevier came back again,
And up the ridge the Britons ran,
  Thinned by the leaden rain.

Relieved by reinforcements,
  They wheeled and charged again,
O'er rock and hillock, log and stone,
  And through the heaps of slain.

On Shelby and on Campbell
  They charged in wrath once more,
Though every step they made in front
  Was in their comrades' gore.

But Cleaveland now had rallied,
  Sevier kept firing fierce,
And through our solid centre there
  They vainly strove to pierce.

Then first there rose our shouting,
  And rang our wild hurra;
For well we knew that they would lose
  And we would win the day.

It roused the Briton's anger,
  Who bade his men stand fast;
And, turning, tried another charge,
  The fourth one and the last.

But now our blood had risen,
  The hour of fury came;
And driving them within their lines,
  We hemmed them round with flame.

The dead lay heaped around us,
  The ground with blood was wet;
And gouts of gore hung dripping there
  From knife and bayonet.

But still our hardy hunters,
  As when the fight began,
Kept plying trigger busily,
  And no one missed his man.

Still smaller grew the circle
  Around the loyal band;
Still fell our long-pent hate upon
  The spoiler of our land.

Hark! Forguson is speaking!
  His voice is stern and low—
"To saddle, horsemen! Sabres draw!
  And charge upon the foe!"

Ah! deadly was that order,
  For, as upon his horse
10

Each horseman strove to mount, he fell
  Or wounded or a corse.

But with his heart undaunted,
  The soldier of the crown
Contrived to save one section there,
  And bade it ride us down.

Down came the bold Dupoister,
  And down came Forguson:
We held our fire, for well we knew
  Our work was nearly done.

Down came they like a torrent—
  A stream of bold and brave;
We met them like the solid rock
  That breaks to foam the wave.

The clinking of their horse-hoofs
  Was only heard at first,
Then came a sound as sharp and loud
  As though a mine had burst;

Down falls both horse and rider,
  Backward the charge rebounds,
And down falls gallant Forguson
  With seven mortal wounds.

The tide was spent and harmless;
  Ere we could fire again,
Up went the white, appealing flag—
  None raised to us in vain.

Up went a cry for quarter,
  And down their muskets fell,
While rang our cry of victory
  Through nook, ravine, and dell.

And so upon King's Mountain,
  From rise till set of sun,
By hardy western mountaineers
  The battle-field was won.

MRS. MERRILL'S DEFENCE.

The event which forms the subject of the ballad occurred in Nelson County, Kentucky, during the summer of 1787. About midnight, the approach of a hostile party was made known to John Merrill and his wife, by the barking of their house-dog. At first, Merrill supposed it to be some travellers seeking shelter, and opened the door. He received the fire of a half-dozen rifles, which broke an arm and a thigh. He fell, and his wife, at his call, closed the door. The Indians broke open the door, but Mrs. Merrill, who was a very large and powerful woman, killed four of them with an axe, and they gave that up. They next climbed the roof to effect an entrance by the broad chimney. There was a fire smouldering on the hearth, and on this Mrs. Merrill threw the feathers of the bed, which she had ripped open. The smoke caused two of the remaining three Indians to fall insensible. Braining these, she ran to the open door where the last surviving savage was entering. He was too close for her to strike, but she cut his cheek with the keen blade of the axe. He gave a yell of affright and despair, and fled, spreading a terrible story of the strength and courage of his female antagonist. A similar instance of female courage is that of Mrs. Dustan, in New England; but in the latter case the victims were asleep.

THE LONG-KNIFE SQUAW.

I was out upon the Piqua, two-and-forty years ago,
Ere my sinews lost their vigor, or my head received its snow.

I was not so skilled in woodcraft as I should have been that day,
And towards the shade of evening, in the forest lost my way.

Yet I wandered hither, thither, till beside a grey old rock,
I beheld the smoky lodges of a band of Shawanock.

There was peace between the races, and a welcome warm I found,
And a supper which they gave me, by the camp-fire, on the ground.

That despatched, I fell to smoking, and as up the round moon rolled,
With a thirsty ear I listened to the tales the old men told.

There they sat and chatted gayly, while the flickering of the blaze
Led the shadows on their faces in a wild and devious maze.

And among them one I noted, unto whom the rest gave place,
Which was token he was foremost in the fight or in the chase.

He had been among the white men till he spoke our language well,
Though his speech was marked by phrases that from Western hunters fell.

There was pausing in the stories, when he turned and spoke to me,
As his red pipe he replenished—"I could tell a tale," said he.

"Those there are of daring white men, whom no danger can appall;
But I knew a squaw among them, who surpassed them one and all.

"Six good Shawanock, my comrades, did that pale-face woman kill."
Then I said—"Pray tell the story!" Quoth the other—"So I will.

"There were seven of us together, who upon an August day,
From the sullen, broad Ohio, up Salt River took our way.

"Up the Rolling Fork we travelled, seeking where we might obtain
Precious plunder from the living, bleeding trophies from the slain.

"By a spring-branch in the bottom, near a clearing in the wood,
Hidden by the sombre hemlocks, Merrill's low-roofed cabin stood.

"It was built of logs of white-oak, chinked, save loop-holes here and there,
With a door of heavy puncheons, made the axe's blow to bear.

"At its end a good stone chimney reared itself among the trees,
And the smoke-wreaths, as we neared it, still were breaking in the breeze.

"Out we lay upon the mountain, till the midnight hour came on,
Till the darkness growing deeper told the summer moon had gone.

"Then we downward crept in silence—not a rustle, scarce a stir—
Till by chance a stone we loosened, which descended with a whirr.

"Rose the dog who had been lying in the cabin's deepest shade,
Snuffed our presence in the valley, and, to warn his master, bayed.

"Then aroused he came to tear us, in his fury, limb from limb,
But my hatchet's blow unerring was enough to quiet him.

"There was stirring in the cabin, and I heard old Merrill say—
'Wife, that is some wearied hunter, who perchance has lost his way.

"'Rouse you, stir the ash-hid embers, and get ready to prepare
Bed of feathers for the stranger and a bait of cabin fare.'

"How we chuckled as he said it; then, in English, 'House!' I cried,
While my comrades all stood ready, when the door should open wide.

"With one hand his rifle grasping, Merrill then unclosed the door,
When we poured a sudden volley, and he sank upon the floor.

"In the fall the gun exploded, lighting up again the dark;
But no fingers drew the trigger, and the bullet found no mark.

"Ere we reached the open portal, though the journey was not far,
Lo! the woman Merrill closed it, and secured it with a bar.

"Long we hacked and long we hammered at the door with useless din,
Till at length a heavy sapling, fiercely driven, burst it in.

"Young Penswataway, our leader, stout old Cornstalk's gallant son,
At the breach we had thus opened, entered in the foremost one.

"He had battled at Point Pleasant, and escaped the deadly ball,
By the weapon of a woman at the dead of night to fall.

"There she stood, that fearless woman, in her hand a heavy axe;
Came a sound of skull-bone crashing, and he died there in his tracks.

"Then, as four more strove to enter at the breach within the door,
One by one my slaughtered comrades sank and died upon the floor.

"Thus that stern unflinching woman managed five of us to slay,
And with axe and blow so ready those surviving kept at bay.

"Yet another entry offered; so, while I with rifle stood,
Lest the woman should escape us in the darkness of the wood,

"To the roof my two companions quickly climbed, a path to gain
By the great, capacious chimney, where resistance would be vain;

" For, so soon as they descended and attacked her on the floor,
Unopposed I'd find an entrance in the then unguarded door.

" But let no one boast his cunning, if a squaw be in the way,
Never fox hath more of shrewdness than a woman held at bay.

" From its place within the corner soon she tore a feather-bed,
And she tossed it in an instant on the embers fiery red.

" Scorched with fierce and sudden blazing, nearly stifled with the smoke,
Fell my two remaining comrades, to receive her axe's stroke.

" Then I struggled at the entrance, and had partly made my way
When the woman came before me, like a wounded buck at bay.

" From her mouth the foam was flying, and her eyes were glazed and
Such a sight to shake my courage, I before had never seen.   [green;

" Turned I quickly in my terror, bounding through the darkness deep,
And I never stopped my running till the dawn began to peep.

" Now, what think you of my story ?" said the savage unto me—
" Was she not a woman worthy leader of a tribe to be ?"

" Ay !" I answered, " but I tell you, should you try it, you would see
We have many a hundred women that in need were stout as she.

" On the mountains of Virginia, in Kentucky's bloody ground,
In the forests of Ohio, scores of such are to be found—

" Women tender, trusting, tearful ; yet if peril forced among,
They can fight as stern and fiercely as a pantheress for her young."

Quoth the chieftain, " If so many like that woman you can find,
You should send them forth to battle, while your men remained behind.

" I have met your braves in combat when the skies were red with fire,
And the sabres of your horsemen flashed the lightning of their ire—

" When your brazen-bodied cannon spoke their wrath to those around,
And the trampling of your legions shook the awed and trembling ground.

" Where the waters of Kanawha rush to join a clearer tide,
I was there with stout old Cornstalk, when you broke our power and pride.

" With the Mingoes, under Girty, at Fort Henry I was one,
When your forty kept four hundred baffled there from sun to sun.

" By Tecumthe's side I battled at the Thames the day he fell,
Where continual flash kept lighting forest, river, swamp, and dell.

" But I never knew a terror, and a fear I never felt,
Save that midnight when the woman so upon my comrades dealt.

" And if I were young and likely, then, whatever dames I saw,
I would wed none save the equal of that daring long-knife squaw."

THERE is no event in American history which seems to be so misunderstood, especially in details, as the battle fought in New Orleans after the close of the war of 1812. The commander of the Americans at that notable repulse became afterwards a prominent politician, or, rath-

ANDREW JACKSON.

er, resumed his political career, and was twice elected President of the United States by the Democratic party, which his course in office aided to disintegrate. The contest during the three times he was a candidate was extremely bitter, and while he was lauded by his friends as a hero, patriot, and statesman, he was denounced by his foes as an illiterate ruffian, ignorant alike of military science and state-craft. The battle upon which his fame mainly rested, was said to have been won entirely by the folly of the British, who stupidly marched upon impregnable works, and were shot down easily by expert marksmen intrenched behind cotton-bales. This last error is amusing, and nothing will ever correct it. The embankment behind which most of the militia lay was formed of swamp-mud mainly, the best material possible for earthworks. A few cotton-bales had been used at one point, but one of them being fired, the dense smoke made it an annoyance, and it was speedily removed. That my readers may comprehend the affair, I give a brief account of the operations leading up to the fight.

The proclamations of Lieutenant-colonel Nichols at Pensacola, which, in violation of Spanish neutrality, he occupied with a British force, and the attempt of the enemy to obtain the aid and co-operation of Lafitte, the head of the Baratarian outlaws, had aroused the attention of Jackson, who acted with his usual promptness and decision, without awaiting orders from the War Department. He had been satisfied of these designs before, through information obtained by means of his agents, and waited an opportunity to strike a blow at the combined British and Spanish enemy. He knew that New Orleans was to be the objective point of an expedition, and prepared for its defence. Recruiting went on slowly; the Southern Indians were openly or covertly hostile ; but the failure of a naval and land attack on Fort Bowyer, repulsed with slaughter, and the loss of the flag-ship, disengaged most of the savages from alliance with Nichols, and brought in large numbers of volunteers. Jackson marched against Pensacola, where the British were intrenched, and proposed to the governor to occupy two of the forts with American garrisons until the Spanish government could send enough troops to make its neutrality respected. This the governor refused, when Jackson at once attacked the town, and after storming a battery, most of the forts were surrendered. Fort Barrancas was in the hands of the British, but before Jackson could attack it, the enemy abandoned and blew it up, and with the Spanish governor and troops embarked on the squadron and left the harbor. The American government gave a cold support, almost amounting to censure, for this necessary and justifiable action ; but public opinion in the South and West sustained the commander of the Seventh Department.

VILLERÉ'S MANSION.

Jackson, who had gone to Mobile before this to look after its defence, received from Governor Claiborne the letter of Lafitte, giving the British propositions and their rejection, and learned that the citizens of New Orleans, under the lead of Edward Livingston, had organized a Defence Committee. He soon after left for New Orleans, where he arrived on the 2d of December. He found the people alarmed and discordant—the masses blaming the Legislature, the Legislature the governor, and the governor both. There was a lack of money, arms, ammunition, and men. It is true there were two militia regiments and a slender volunteer battalion, commanded by Major Planché, a brave creole officer ;* but these were not sufficient to guard the

---

* Creole meant originally the native-born descendant of foreign white parents. It is now applied to the native whites in Louisiana. People outside of that state frequently misapprehend its meaning, and think the word denotes mixed blood.

city, which contained a large amount of property, and had but meagre fortifications to protect its approaches. Jackson went actively to work to improve the condition of things by strengthening the forts, erecting new ones, obstructing the bayous, and establishing discipline.

"THE HERMITAGE," JACKSON'S RESIDENCE, IN 1861.

On the 9th of December the British squadron, having on board over seven thousand troops, made their appearance and anchored near the entrance to Lake Borgne. Here they prepared to land. They were not aware of the revelations of Lafitte, and hoped to take the place by surprise. They soon learned their error. The late commodore (then lieutenant) Ap Catesby Jones was in command of our flotilla, and had sent out two gun-boats, under command of Lieutenant M'Keever and sailing-master Ulrick, to watch their approach. These reported the fleet to Jones on the 10th, and Jones made for Pass Christian, where the astounded enemy saw his flotilla at anchor on the 13th. As it was impossible to land troops under these circumstances, Admiral Cochrane manned sixty barges, each armed with a carronade and filled with men, to capture the tiny squadron, which was manned by one hundred and eighty-three men. He succeeded in this, with the loss of three hundred killed and wounded, after an hour's fight. The American loss was only six killed and thirty-five wounded. This partly cleared the way for the enemy, who also discovered the passage through the Bayou Bienvenu. On the 22d, as many of the invaders as could find transportation embarked, and landing at the Fisherman's Village, at the mouth of the bayou, captured most of the picket-guard. The men taken so represented the numbers of Jackson's force that the invaders proceeded with more caution. They moved slowly up the bayou, and at Villeré's plantation surrounded the house, and took Major Villeré, the commander of the pickets. He escaped, however, and carried the news to Jackson.

The American general in the mean while had not been idle. He had proclaimed martial law in the city, brought the troops to a state of discipline, infused his heroic spirit into the population, and sent messengers to Coffee, Carroll, and Thomas, urging them to move forward their commands as soon as possible. On the 22d, Carroll's troops of Tennessee levies, all skilled riflemen, landed in New Orleans, and Coffee's brigade of mounted rifles were encamped five miles above the city. As soon as the news of the enemy's presence was brought to Jackson he determined to attack on the night of the 23d, both to check the enemy and to familiarize his raw troops with their work. In the mean time the schooner *Carolina* was directed to drop down the river in the darkness, and open fire on the enemy's camp. That fire would drive them upon the land-forces.

The affair was carefully managed and brilliantly carried out. The British were driven under the levee, and the troops, excited and triumphant, returned to the city in perfect order and with full confidence in their commander.

The events of the night had somewhat depressed the spirits of the enemy, and on Christmas-day, which was cold and disagreeable, a gloom pervaded the British encampment. That day, however, their spirits were lifted by the arrival of Sir Edward Pakenham, "the hero of Salamanca." Sir Edward was then in the prime of manhood, thirty-three years of age, brave, upright, and honorable, and altogether undeserving of the obloquy that so long hung over his memory as the reputed author of the asserted watchword—"beauty and booty." He was among old friends, most of the troops there having fought with him in the Spanish Peninsula. He gave renewed life to the force. A battery of twelve and eighteen pounders and a howitzer was planted so as to command the *Carolina*, and by means of hot shot, on the night of the 27th, she was set on fire and destroyed. The *Louisiana*, the only remaining American vessel, escaped with difficulty. Pakenham arranged his army in two columns, one under Keane and the other under Gibbs, and moved forward, driving in the American outposts, and then encamped during the night, where the riflemen annoyed them and prevented them from much sleep. The next morn-

JACKSON'S TOMB.

ing at dawn they moved to the attack, two to one in numbers and confident of success. But they met with an unexpected resistance. The Baratarians and the crew of the *Carolina* came up, and opened on them with twenty-four pounders, while the fire of the *Louisiana* from the river enfiladed their line, doing terrible damage. On the right, Gibbs was not more successful, though less terribly punished, and Pakenham was compelled to order a retreat, which on the left

PLAIN OF CHALMETTE.—BATTLE-GROUND.

became disorderly. The comparative loss was remarkable—the Americans had seventeen killed and wounded, and the British about one hundred and fifty—owing, doubtless, to the terrible oblique fire of the *Louisiana*.

At the council of war called that evening, it was determined to land heavy siege guns from the ships, to throw up redoubts, and prepare for a regular and concerted attack. During the next few days this was carried out, and several attempts were made to break the American line. The fighting went on, until Sir Edward, finding he could make no impression, concluded to hazard all in a stroke and carry the works by storm.

JOHN COFFEE.

Jackson during all this time was energetically at work strengthening his position. On the 4th of January his forces were increased by the arrival of General Thomas, with two thousand drafted men from Kentucky, raw and undisciplined, but for defensive work useful, being cool, brave, and good marksmen. His intrenchments were carried into the swamp to prevent being flanked, and batteries were placed in proper positions on the lines on both sides of the river. Behind the levee on Jourdan's plantation, Commander Patterson had placed a battery of heavy guns from his schooner, and manned them with seamen. This battery commanding the front of the American lines, drove the enemy from Chalmette's plantation to a point between Bienvenu and De la Ronde's.

On the 7th Major-general Lambert arrived with reinforcements, among the rest Sir Edward's own regiment, the 7th Fusileers, bringing his force up to ten thousand men, the very flower of the British army. This was divided into three brigades, commanded by Generals Lambert, Gibbs, and Keane, and on the following morning an attack was to be made on both sides of the Mississippi. Thornton was to cross the river, and fall upon the Americans on that side before dawn. His guns were to be the signal for the main attack. He was detained, however, in the river, and the main attack was not made until daylight. Thornton was quite successful, but retreated when he learned of the terrible repulse on the other side of the river.

The incidents of the main attack and the results will be found in the ballad.

STATUE OF JACKSON IN FRONT OF THE CATHEDRAL.

THE BATTLE OF NEW ORLEANS.

Here, in my rude log cabin,
　Few poorer men there be
Among the mountain ranges
　Of Eastern Tennessee.
My limbs are weak and shrunken,
　White hairs upon my brow,
My dog—lie still, old fellow!—
　My sole companion now.

Yet I, when young and lusty,
   Have gone through stirring scenes,
For I went down with Carroll
   To fight at New Orleans.

You say. you'd like to hear me
   The stirring story tell,
Of those who stood the battle
   And those who fighting fell.
Short work to count our losses—
   We stood and dropped the foe
As easily as by firelight
   Men shoot the buck or doe.
And while they fell by hundreds
   Upon the bloody plain,
Of us, fourteen were wounded
   And only eight were slain.

The eighth of January,
   Before the break of day,
Our raw and hasty levies
   Were brought into array.
No cotton-bales before us—
   Some fool that falsehood told ;
Before us was an earthwork
   Built from the swampy mould.
And there we stood in silence,
   And waited with a frown,
To greet with bloody welcome
   The bull-dogs of the Crown.

The heavy fog of morning
   Still hid the plain from sight,
When came a thread of scarlet
   Marked faintly in the white.
We fired a single cannon,
   And as its thunders rolled,
The mist before us lifted
   In many a heavy fold—
The mist before us lifted
   And in their bravery fine

Came rushing to their ruin
  The fearless British line.

Then from our waiting cannon
  Leaped forth the deadly flame,
To meet the advancing columns
  That swift and steady came.
The thirty-twos of Crowley
  And Bluchi's twenty-four
To Spotts's eighteen-pounders
  Responded with their roar,
Sending the grape-shot deadly
  That marked its pathway plain,
And paved the road it travelled
  With corpses of the slain.

Our rifles firmly grasping,
  And heedless of the din,
We stood in silence waiting
  For orders to begin.
Our fingers on the triggers,
  Our hearts, with anger stirred,
Grew still more fierce and eager
  As Jackson's voice was heard:
"Stand steady! Waste no powder!
  Wait till your shots will tell!
To-day the work you finish—
  See that you do it well!"

Their columns drawing nearer,
  We felt our patience tire,
When came the voice of Carroll,
  Distinct and measured, "Fire!"
Oh! then you should have marked us
  Our volleys on them pour—
Have heard our joyous rifles
  Ring sharply through the roar,
And seen their foremost columns
  Melt hastily away
As snow in mountain gorges
  Before the floods of May.

They soon re-formed their columns,
  And, 'mid the fatal rain
We never ceased to hurtle,
  Came to their work again.
The Forty-fourth is with them,
  That first its laurels won
With stout old Abercrombie
  Beneath an eastern sun.
It rushes to the battle,
  And, though within the rear
Its leader is a laggard,
  It shows no signs of fear.

It did not need its colonel,
  For soon there came instead
An eagle-eyed commander,
  And on its march he led.
'Twas Pakenham in person,
  The leader of the field;
I knew it by the cheering
  That loudly round him pealed;
And by his quick, sharp movement
  We felt his heart was stirred,
As when at Salamanca
  He led the fighting Third.

I raised my rifle quickly,
  I sighted at his breast,
God save the gallant leader
  And take him to his rest!
I did not draw the trigger,
  I could not for my life.
So calm he sat his charger
  Amid the deadly strife,
That in my fiercest moment
  A prayer arose from me—
God save that gallant leader,
  Our foeman though he be!

Sir Edward's charger staggers;
  He leaps at once to ground.

And ere the beast falls bleeding
  Another horse is found.
His right arm falls—'tis wounded ;
  He waves on high his left ;
In vain he leads the movement,
  The ranks in twain are cleft.
The men in scarlet waver
  Before the men in brown,
And fly in utter panic—
  The soldiers of the Crown !

I thought the work was over,
  But nearer shouts were heard,
And came, with Gibbs to head it,
  The gallant Ninety-third.
Then Pakenham, exulting,
  With proud and joyous glance,
Cried, " Children of the tartan—
  Bold Highlanders—advance !
Advance to scale the breastworks,
  And drive them from their hold,
And show the stainless courage
  That marked your sires of old !"

His voice as yet was ringing,
  When, quick as light, there came
The roaring of a cannon,
  And earth seemed all aflame.
Who causes thus the thunder
  The doom of men to speak ?
It is the Baratarian,
  The fearless Dominique.
Down through the marshalled Scotsmen
  The step of death is heard,
And by the fierce tornado
  Falls half the Ninety-third.

The smoke passed slowly upward,
  And, as it soared on high,
I saw the brave commander
  In dying anguish lie.

11

They bear him from the battle
  Who never fled the foe;
Unmoved by death around them
  His bearers softly go.
In vain their care, so gentle,
  Fades earth and all its scenes;
The man of Salamanca
  Lies dead at New Orleans.

But where were his lieutenants?
  Had they in terror fled?
No! Keane was sorely wounded
  And Gibbs as good as dead.
Brave Wilkinson commanding,
  A major of brigade,
The shattered force to rally
  A final effort made.
He led it up our ramparts,
  Small glory did he gain—
Our captives some; some slaughtered,
  And he himself was slain.

The stormers had retreated,
  The bloody work was o'er;
The feet of the invaders
  Were soon to leave our shore.
We rested on our rifles
  And talked about the fight,
When came a sudden murmur
  Like fire from left to right;
We turned and saw our chieftain,
  And then, good friend of mine,
You should have heard the cheering
  That rang along the line.

For well our men remembered
  How little, when they came,
Had they but native courage,
  And trust in Jackson's name;
How through the day he labored,
  How kept the vigils still,

Till discipline controlled us—
  A stronger power than will ;
And how he hurled us at them
  Within the evening hour,
That red night in December,
  And made us feel our power.

In answer to our shouting
  Fire lit his eye of grey ;
Erect, but thin and pallid,
  He passed upon his bay.
Weak from the baffled fever,
  And shrunken in each limb,
The swamps of Alabama
  Had done their work on him ;
But spite of that and fasting,
  And hours of sleepless care,
The soul of Andrew Jackson
  Shone forth in glory there.

THE continually triumphant march of the American troops, under Scott, from Vera Cruz to the City of Mexico, in spite of greater numbers of opposing soldiers, fighting for their own soil, led many to undervalue the courage and endurance of the enemy. There never was a more signal error. The Mexicans fought fiercely and well; they displayed daring and steadiness, though they were not always able to stand before the bayonet, to whose uses they had not been trained. Their signal defeats, occurring after obstinate and bloody resistance, were due to the inefficiency of their general officers. Properly headed the Mexicans would make as fine soldiers as any in the world.

Among the successive battles which marked the invasion, that of *El Molino del Rey* (The King's Mill) was one of the most spirit-stirring. One of the objects of attack consisted of a range of buildings, five hundred feet in front and well fortified, known by the title of the poem. On the left and farther off was the *Casamata* or arsenal, loop-holed, and surrounded by a quadrangular field-work. Ravines and ditches, irregularities of ground, the position of the Mexican troops, and their superiority in numbers, made the task exceedingly difficult. The attack was begun at daylight. The enemy fought desperately and bitterly. Carrying the Mexican guns in the open field, the Americans were driven back with great slaughter, but with sufficient support retook them. At right and left the battle raged with a fury that showed the courage and perseverance of both sides. The intrenchments were stormed, but not until after a severe contest, and until house after house within the intrenchments had been broken into, the Mexicans everywhere making a heroic resistance. The loss on both sides was heavy.

BATTLE OF THE KING'S MILL.

Said my landlord, white-headed Gil Gomez,
  With newspaper held in his hand—
"So they've built from El Paso a railway
  That Yankees may visit our land.
As guests let them come and be welcome,
  But not as they came here before;
They are rather rough fellows to handle
  In the rush of the battle and roar.

"They took Vera Cruz and its castle;
  In triumph they marched through the land;
We fought them with desperate daring,
  But lacked the right man to command.

They stormed, at a loss, Cerro Gordo—
  Every mile in their movement it cost;
And when they arrived at Puebla,
  Some thousands of men they had lost.

"Ere our capital fell, and the city
  By foreign invaders was won,
We called out among its defenders
  Each man who could handle a gun.
Chapultepec stood in their pathway;
  Churubusco they had to attack;
The Mill of the King—well, I fought there,
  And they were a hard nut to crack.

"While their right was assailing the ramparts,
  Our force struck their left on the field,
Where our colonel, in language that stirred us,
  To love of our country appealed.
And we swore that we never would falter
  Before either sabre or ball;
We would beat back the foeman before us,
  Or dead on the battle-field fall.

"Fine words, you may say, but we meant them;
  And so when they came up the hill
We poured on them volley on volley,
  And riddled their ranks with a will.
Their line in a moment was broken;
  They closed it, and came with a cheer;
But still we fired quickly and deadly,
  And felt neither pity nor fear.

"We smote the blue column with grape-shot,
  But it rushed as the wild torrent runs;
At the pieces they slew our best gunners,
  And took in the struggle our guns.
We sprang in a rage to retake them,
  And lost nearly half of our men;
Then, baffled and beaten, retreated,
  And gained our position again.

" Ceased their yell, and in spite of our firing
    They dressed like an arrow their line,
Then, standing there moveless a moment,
    Their eyes flashed with purpose malign,
All still as the twilight in summer,
    No cloud on the sky to deform,

THE LAST CHARGE.

Like the lull in the voices of nature
  Ere wakens the whirlwind and storm.

"We had fought them with death-daring spirit,
  And courage unyielding till then ;
No man could have forced us to falter,
  But these were more demons than men.
Our ranks had been torn by their bullets,
  We filled all the gaps they had made ;
But the pall o that terrible silence
  The hearts of our boldest dismayed.

"Before us no roaring of cannon,
  Rifle-rattle, or musketry peal ;
But there on the ocean of battle
  Surged steady the billow of steel.
Fierce we opened our fire on the column,
  We pierced it with ball here and there ;
But it swept on in pitiless sternness
  Till we faltered and fled in despair.

"After that all their movements were easy ;
  At their storming Chapultepec fell,
And that ended the war—we were beaten :
  No story is left me to tell.
And now they come back to invade us,
  Though not with the bullet and blade ;
They are here with their goods on a railway,
  To conquer the country by trade."

THE story that follows is, as the old magazines used to say of their tales, "founded on fact." The foundation is rather slender. Similar incidents have occurred in all wars, ancient and modern; and nothing delights the old soldier more, when peace comes, than to meet a former antagonist, who, as in this instance, has "proved worthy of his steel."

THE FENCING-MASTER.

You wish to improve yourself? Good! There's a tool;
Let us see of what stuff you are made; and—keep cool.
Never hurry. On guard! When I thrust, parry so.
Longe! Gracious! Disarmed me! Well, this is a go.
"An accident?" Make me think that, if you can.
You had better give lessons than take them, young man.
Wrist of steel, form of whalebone, keen-eyed, supple, tall—
You could manage that cut-and-thrust there on the wall.

"A Toledo!" No doubt of it; here on the blade
Is the name of the Spaniard by whom it was made,
And the place where they forged it; its metal can tell
It was made where such weapons they fashioned right well;
But that, after all, has slight interest—I
Well know how I got it, the where and the why;
And thence comes a story—a memory, too.
Will I tell it? Why, yes, I don't care if I do.

I was merely lieutenant—I never wore stars,
Though it rained brigadiers at the time; and my scars
Were got in the hours when I fought on my feet,
And lucky to keep them at moments when sleet
From some thousands of muskets upon us fell fast,
And each breath that we drew seemed like drawing the last,
And the foeman kept plying his bullets and shell,
And to right and to left comrades they staggered and fell.

'Twas at Fredericksburg Heights, where we charged like such fools,
And learned by experience—that saddest of schools—
An experience that brought us a fire-rain beneath—
Not to crack a hard nut, nor to try, with our teeth,
That I got this old sabre, and with it a scar,
From a small pistol bullet, my beauty to mar;
And a narrow escape, for an inch t'other way,
And a narrow earth-jacket I'd worn the next day.

I hated the enemy, then—no offence,
If you held 'tother side, each man acts on his sense—
And I thought they were wrong, as I thought we were right;
No doubt they thought otherwise. And they could fight.
No man can deny it; and there well intrenched
They awaited our coming, while none of us blenched,
Though we knew it was madness to charge up that hill,
That a child might have held had it courage and will.

At the word we were off. It was glorious to see
How we marched to the charge with a step fast and free.
Flags flying, throats cheering, and every rank dressed
To an inch in its straightness; when quick from the crest
Opened loudly a hundred of cannon or more,
And the path of the balls was mapped out in our gore.
We were brave, but some tasks are too fearful for man;
We faltered, we turned—who could help it?—we ran.

We tried it again with another rebuff;
And again, till we found we'd been hammered enough;
And then by the river at close of the day,
With the wounded, the men who came out of the fray—
And I tell you right glad to be certainly back—
Lay there on the ground. 'Twas a mournful bivouac,
With few of us sure as we talked o'er our loss
If they'd suffer us safely the river to cross.

I strolled out to the picket—some thirty were there,
With their arms in good order, their eyeballs kept bare—
When, an hour before midnight, there came quick and hard
The trample of horse charging down on the guard;

And we met them—a squadron of dare-devils they—
But a sharp edge of bayonets kept them at bay,
While we emptied some barrels, with never a corse,
Though we wounded one rider and crippled his horse.

The rider pitched over; his comrades they heard
His yell as he fell; but they turned and they spurred,
For by this time our camp was aroused and poured in,
And the visitors stayed not their laurels to win;
When what does this Hotspur but spring to his feet,
And, ready a regiment singly to meet,
Draw weapon, and there, right in front of our line,
To guard bring his sabre, and cross it with mine.

'Twas a regular duel: our men gathered round;
Save the clash of the blades there was never a sound.
'Twas cut, thrust, and parry—the fellow fenced well—
But at last on his shoulder a heavy blow fell,
And his sword dropped to earth—in an instant he felt
With his left for a pistol that hung at his belt,
And he fired. O'er my temple the ball ploughed its track,
When I tripped him, and threw my bold youth on his back.

I said as I held him, "This rage has no use;
You're two-thirds a lion and one-third a goose.
Do you want to fight armies! This passes a joke;
Surrender at once, or your throttle I'll choke.
Stop the struggling, my madman, and tell us your choice—"
"I give my parole." 'Twas a musical voice,
With a rather thin treble. Conceive my annoy
When I found I had wasted my strength on a boy.

'Twas a boy of sixteen, with his lip free of down,
Whose ball cut a groove 'twixt my temple and crown,
And who handled his sabre as deftly and keen
As a master of fence. Yes, a boy of sixteen.
And I said, as I looked on him there where he stood,
Defiant, though conquered, and dauntless in mood,
"You crow well, my cockerel, ere you have spurs;
Has your mother more such in that rare brood of hers?"

Then he laughed, and his forefinger rose, as he said,
" You carry the mark of my spur on your head—
Who'll give me a drink?" as at word of command
A dozen canteens were thrust ready to hand ;
But ere he could choose, from his features there shrank
The blood till he paled, then he staggered and sank.
We raised him ; I stooped there and pillowed his head
On my knee ; and I shivered—I thought he was dead.

But no, sir, he rallied. We bore him away,
When we crossed o'er the river, ere break of the day,
Where our surgeon soon healed up his wound, and I nursed
The boy, and grew fond where I'd liked from the first,
Till, ready for prison, but hating confine,
He fled one dark night and got over the line ;
And I never laid eyes on my bold shaver since.
That's his sword, and a weapon would honor a prince.

You smile at the story—I've seen you, but where ?
What name did you carry? "George Gaston!"—well—there !
Let me grapple your fist, boy? I'd never have known
You, with all of those whiskers. Why, how you have grown !
Twelve years ! well, it *does* make a difference, I see,
In you, as it probably *has* made in me.
I can't tell how glad I'm to see you at last.
Sit down ; take a pipe ; and we'll talk o'er the past.

AN AMBUSCADE.

The incident which gave rise to the following poem happened about 1861, in Western Virginia, somewhere in the Gauley River region. The story may be correct, or not. I do not vouch for its accuracy. At all events, I have considered it to be *si non e vero, e ben trovato*, as the Italian proverb has it. If it be not true, it is well feigned.

THE CHARGE BY THE FORD.

Eighty and nine with their captain
  Rode on the enemy's track,
Rode in the grey of the morning:
  Nine of the ninety came back.

Slow rose the mist from the river,
  Lighter each moment the way;
Careless and tearless and fearless
  Galloped they on to the fray.

Singing in tune, how the scabbard
  Loud on the stirrup-irons rang,
Clinked as the men rose in saddle,
  Fell as they sank with a clang!

What is it moves by the river,
  Faded and weary and weak?
Grey-backs—a cross on their banner—
  Yonder the foe whom they seek.

Silence! They see not, they hear not,
  Tarrying there by the marge;
Forward! Draw sabre! Trot! Gallop!
  Charge like a hurricane! Charge!

Ah! 'twas a man-trap infernal;
　Fire like the deep pit of hell!
Volley on volley to meet them,
　Mixed with the grey rebels' yell.

Ninety had ridden to battle,
　Tracing the enemy's track;
Ninety had ridden to battle,
　Nine of the ninety came back.

Honor the nine of the ninety,
　Honor the heroes who came
Scathless from nine hundred muskets,
　Safe from the lead-bearing flame.

Eighty and one of the troopers
　Lie on the field of the slain—
Lie on the red field of honor:
　Honor the nine who remain.

Cold are the dead there, and gory,
　There where their life-blood was spilt;
Back come the living, each sabre
　Red from the point to the hilt.

Give them three cheers and a tiger!
　Let the flags wave as they come!
Give them the blare of the trumpet!
　Give them the roll of the drum!

THE following is an attempt to add one more to the few patriotic songs of the country. What-ever may be said of the words, the melody and the music are undoubtedly marked by spirit and vigor.

FLAG OF THE RAINBOW.

PATRIOTIC SONG—SOLO AND CHORUS (MIXED VOICES).

WORDS BY THOMAS DUNN ENGLISH.   MUSIC COMPOSED BY MAX BRAUN.

Ensign, whose story is re-cord of glo-ry—Flag of the rainbow and banner of stars.

D. S. S: 3d time (Fine.)

Flag of a land where the people are free,
　　Ever the breezes salute and caress it ;
Planted on earth, or afloat on the sea,
　　Gallant men guard it, and fair women bless it.
Fling out its folds o'er a country united,
Warmed by the fires that our forefathers lighted,
Refuge where down-trodden man is invited—
　　Flag of the rainbow and banner of stars.
　　　　Chorus.—Flag of the rainbow, etc.

Flag that our sires gave in trust to their sons,
　　Symbol and sign of a liberty glorious,
While the grass grows, and the clear water runs,
　　Ever invincible, ever victorious.
Long may it 'waken our pride and devotion,
Rippling its colors in musical motion,
First on the land and supreme on the ocean—
　　Flag of the rainbow and banner of stars.
　　　　Chorus.—Flag of the rainbow, etc.

The Orchestra Music (eight Instruments) can be had from the Composer, at Newark, N. J.

SELECTED HOME READING.

Carleton's Poetical Works.
Illustrated. Square 8vo, Ornamental Cloth, $2 00; Gilt Edges, $2 50.

FARM BALLADS. By WILL CARLETON.

FARM LEGENDS. By WILL CARLETON.

FARM FESTIVALS. By WILL CARLETON.

CITY BALLADS. By WILL CARLETON.

YOUNG FOLKS' CENTENNIAL RHYMES. By WILL CARLETON. Illustrated. Post 8vo, Cloth, $1 50.

English's Poetical Works.
THE BOY'S BOOK OF BATTLE LYRICS. By THOMAS DUNN ENGLISH, M.D., LL.D. Illustrated. Square 8vo, Ornamental Cloth. (*Just Ready.*)

AMERICAN BALLADS. By THOMAS DUNN ENGLISH, M.D., LL.D. 32mo, Paper, 25 cents; Cloth, 40 cents.

Harper's Cyclopædia of British and American Poetry.
Harper's Cyclopædia of British and American Poetry. Edited by EPES SARGENT. Large 8vo, Illuminated Cloth, Colored Edges, $4 50.

Poets of the Nineteenth Century.
Poets of the Nineteenth Century. Selected and Edited by the Rev. ROBERT ARIS WILLMOTT. With English and American Additions, arranged by EVERT A. DUYCKINCK. New and Enlarged Edition. Superbly illustrated with 141 Engravings. In elegant small 4to form, printed on Superfine Tinted Paper, richly bound in Extra Cloth, Bevelled, Gilt Edges, $5 00; Half Calf, $5 50; Full Turkey Morocco, $9 00.

The Poets and Poetry of Scotland.
From the Earliest to the Present Time. Comprising Characteristic Selections from the Works of the more Noteworthy Scottish Poets, with Biographical and Critical Notices. By JAMES GRANT WILSON. With Portraits on Steel. 2 vols., 8vo, Cloth, $10 00; Cloth, Gilt Edges, $11 00; Half Calf, $14 50; Full Morocco, $18 00.

Friendly Edition of Shakespeare's Works.
Edited by W. J. ROLFE. In 20 volumes. Illustrated. 16mo, Sheets, $27 00; Cloth, $30 00; Half Calf, $60 00. (*In a Box.*)

Shakspeare's Dramatic Works.
The Dramatic Works of Shakspeare, with the Corrections and Illustrations of Dr. JOHNSON, G. STEEVENS, and others. Revised by ISAAC REED. Illustrated. 6 vols., Royal 12mo, Cloth, $9 00; Sheep, $11 40.

Rolfe's English Classics.

Edited, with Notes, by W. J. ROLFE, A.M. Illustrated. Small 4to, Flexible Cloth, 56 cents per volume; Paper, 40 cents per volume.

SELECT POEMS OF GOLDSMITH.—SELECT POEMS OF THOMAS GRAY.

SHAKESPEARE'S THE TEMPEST.—MERCHANT OF VENICE.—KING HENRY THE EIGHTH.—JULIUS CÆSAR.—RICHARD THE SECOND.—MACBETH.—MIDSUMMER NIGHT'S DREAM.—KING HENRY THE FIFTH.—KING JOHN.—AS YOU LIKE IT.—KING HENRY IV. Part I.—KING HENRY IV. Part II.—HAMLET.—MUCH ADO ABOUT NOTHING.—ROMEO AND JULIET.—OTHELLO.—TWELFTH NIGHT.—THE WINTER'S TALE.—RICHARD THE THIRD.—KING LEAR.—ALL'S WELL THAT ENDS WELL.—CORIOLANUS.—TAMING OF THE SHREW.—CYMBELINE.—THE COMEDY OF ERRORS.—ANTONY AND CLEOPATRA.—MEASURE FOR MEASURE.—MERRY WIVES OF WINDSOR.—LOVE'S LABOUR'S LOST.—TIMON OF ATHENS.—TWO GENTLEMEN OF VERONA.—TROILUS AND CRESSIDA.—HENRY VI. Part I.—HENRY VI. Part II.—HENRY VI. Part III.—PERICLES, PRINCE OF TYRE.—THE TWO NOBLE KINSMEN.—VENUS AND ADONIS, &c.—SONNETS.—TITUS ANDRONICUS.

Folk-Lore of Shakespeare.

By the Rev. T. F. THISELTON DYER, M.A., Oxon. 8vo, Cloth, $2 50.

Shakspere: A Critical Study of his Mind and Art.

By EDWARD DOWDEN, LL.D., Vice-President of "The New Shakspere Society." 12mo, Cloth, $1 75.

The Works of Oliver Goldsmith.

Edited by PETER CUNNINGHAM, F.S.A. From New Electrotype Plates. 4 vols., 8vo, Cloth, Paper Labels, Uncut Edges and Gilt Tops, $8 00; Sheep, $10 00; Half Calf, $17 00.

Swinton's Studies in English Literature.

Studies in English Literature: being Typical Selections of British and American Authorship, from Shakespeare to the Present Time; together with Definitions, Notes, Analyses, and Glossary, as an aid to Systematic Literary Study. By Professor WILLIAM SWINTON, A.M., Author of "Harper's Language Series." With Portraits. Crown 8vo, Cloth, $1 50.

Tennyson's Songs, with Music.

Songs from the Published Writings of Alfred Tennyson. Set to Music by various Composers. Edited by W. G. CUSINS. With Portrait and Original Illustrations by Winslow Homer, C. S. Reinhart, A. Fredericks, and Jessie Curtis. Royal 4to, Cloth, Gilt Edges, $5 00.

Complete Works of Alfred, Lord Tennyson,

Poet-Laureate. With an Introductory Sketch by ANNE THACKERAY RITCHIE. With Portraits and Illustrations. Pages 430. 8vo, Cloth, $2 00; Gilt Edges, $2 50.

English Men of Letters. Edited by John Morley.

12mo, Cloth, 75 cents a volume. (*Volumes now ready.*)

JOHNSON. By Leslie Stephen.—GIBBON. By J. C. Morison.—SCOTT. By R. H. Hutton.—SHELLEY. By John Addington Symonds.—HUME. By Professor Huxley.—GOLDSMITH. By William Black.—DEFOE. By William Minto.—BURNS. By Principal Shairp.—SPENSER. By Dean Church.—THACKERAY. By Anthony Trollope.—BURKE. By John Morley.—MILTON. By Mark Pattison.—SOUTHEY. By Edward Dowden.—CHAUCER. By Adolphus William Ward.—BUNYAN. By James Anthony Froude.—COWPER. By Goldwin Smith.—POPE. By Leslie Stephen.—BYRON. By John Nichol.—LOCKE. By Thomas Fowler.—WORDSWORTH. By F. W. H. Myers.—DRYDEN. By G. Saintsbury.—HAWTHORNE. By Henry James, Jr.—LANDOR. By Sidney Colvin.—DE QUINCEY. By David Masson.—LAMB. By Alfred Ainger.—BENTLEY. By R. C. Jebb.—DICKENS. By A. W. Ward.—GRAY. By E. W. Gosse.—SWIFT. By Leslie Stephen.—STERNE. By H. D. Traill.—MACAULAY. By James Cotter Morison.—FIELDING. By Austin Dobson.—SHERIDAN. By Mrs. Oliphant.—ADDISON. By W. J. Courthope.—BACON. By R. W. Church, Dean of St. Paul's.—COLERIDGE. By H. D. Traill. (*Other volumes in preparation.*)

Some Issues in Harper's Half-Hour Series.

GOLDSMITH'S PLAYS. 32mo, Paper, 25 cents; Cloth, 40 cents.

GOLDSMITH'S POEMS. 32mo, Paper, 20 cents; Cloth, 35 cents.

SHERIDAN'S PLAYS.
THE RIVALS and THE SCHOOL FOR SCANDAL. Comedies. By RICHARD BRINSLEY SHERIDAN. 32mo, Paper, 25 cents; Cloth, 40 cents.

COWPER'S TASK. A Poem in Six Books. By WILLIAM COWPER. 32mo, Paper, 20 cents; Cloth, 35 cents.

SIR WALTER SCOTT'S POEMS.
THE LAY OF THE LAST MINSTREL. 32mo, Paper, 20 cents; Cloth, 35 cents.
THE LADY OF THE LAKE. 32mo, Paper, 25 cents; Cloth, 40 cents.
MARMION. 32mo, Paper, 25 cents; Cloth, 40 cents.

BALLADS OF BATTLE AND BRAVERY. Selected by W. G. M'CABE. 32mo, Paper, 25 cents; Cloth, 40 cents.

LITERATURE SERIES. By EUGENE LAWRENCE. In Seven Volumes. 32mo, Paper, 25 cents each; Cloth, 40 cents each.
AMERICAN LITERATURE.—ENGLISH LITERATURE. Romance Period.—Classical Period.—Modern Period.—MEDIÆVAL LITERATURE.—LATIN LITERATURE.—GREEK LITERATURE.

GERMAN LITERATURE. By HELEN S. CONANT. 32mo, Paper, 25 cents; Cloth, 40 cents.

SPANISH LITERATURE. By HELEN S. CONANT. 32mo, Paper, 25 cents; Cloth, 40 cents.

Bayne's Lessons From My Masters.

Lessons from My Masters : Carlyle, Tennyson, and Ruskin. By PETER BAYNE, M.A., LL.D. 12mo, Cloth, $1 75.

English Literature in the Eighteenth Century.

By THOMAS SERGEANT PERRY. 12mo, Cloth, $2 00.

Coleridge's Ancient Mariner. Illustrated by Doré.

The Rime of the Ancient Mariner. By SAMUEL TAYLOR COLERIDGE. Illustrated by GUSTAVE DORÉ. Folio, Cloth, $10 00.

Poe's Raven. Illustrated by Doré.

The Raven. By EDGAR ALLAN POE. Illustrated by GUSTAVE DORÉ. With Comment by E. C. STEDMAN. Folio (Uniform with Doré's *Ancient Mariner*), Illuminated Cloth, Gilt Edges, and in a neat Box, $10 00.

Herrick's Poems. Illustrated by Abbey.

Selections from the Poetry of Robert Herrick. With Drawings by ED- WIN A. ABBEY. 4to, Illuminated Cloth, Gilt Edges, $7 50. (*In a Box.*)

The Book of Gold, and other Poems.

By J. T. TROWBRIDGE. Ill'd. 8vo, Ornamental Covers, Gilt Edges, $2 50.

Halpine's (Miles O'Reilly) Poems.

With a Biographical Sketch and Explanatory Notes. Edited by ROB- ERT B. ROOSEVELT. Portrait on Steel. Post 8vo, Cloth, $2 50.

Symonds's Works.

STUDIES OF THE GREEK POETS. By J. A. SYMONDS. Revised and En- larged by the Author. In two Volumes. Square 16mo, Cloth, $3 50.
SKETCHES AND STUDIES IN SOUTHERN EUROPE. By J. A. SYMONDS. In two Volumes. Post 8vo, Cloth, $4 00.

Mahaffy's Greek Literature.

A History of Classical Greek Literature. By J. P. MAHAFFY. 2 vols., 12mo, Cloth, $4 00.

Simcox's Latin Literature.

A History of Latin Literature, from Ennius to Boethius. By GEORGE AUGUSTUS SIMCOX, M.A. In Two Volumes. 12mo, Cloth, $4 00.

Deshler's Afternoons with the Poets.

Afternoons with the Poets. By C. D. DESHLER. 16mo, Cloth, $1 75.

Songs of Our Youth.

Set to Music. By Miss MULOCK. Square 4to, Cloth, $2 50.

Our Children's Songs. Illustrated.

Selected and Arranged by the Rev. S. IRENÆUS PRIME, D.D. 8vo, Cloth, $1 00.

PUBLISHED BY HARPER & BROTHERS, NEW YORK.

☞ HARPER & BROTHERS *will send any of the foregoing works by mail, postage prepaid, to any part of the United States or Canada, on receipt of the price.*

www.ingramcontent.com/pod-product-compliance
Lightning Source LLC
Chambersburg PA
CBHW032011060726
47497CB00017B/2934